ANJIE, PAT AND INDIA'S POOR

A Collection of Short Stories

MRUTYUNJAY SARANGI

INDIA • SINGAPORE • MALAYSIA

CONTENTS

PREFACE

In November 2021 I had to spend a week in a hospital after testing positive for Covid19. It was quite disconcerting to be in a hospital, with occasional wails piercing the silent night, perhaps announcing the departure of yet another soul on a journey to the unknown. I felt awfully lonely. Nights were spent in sleepless agony, days in restless worry. I wished I had a few good books to read. And I realised, not for the first time, books were a soothing balm for lonely beings. I pledged to God that if I survived, I would convert my hundred-odd stories into collections and dedicate them to those dear souls who crave for a book in their lonely hours.

So, last year I self-published two collections of my short stories – The Jasmine Girl at Haji Ali and A Train to Kolkata. A year later, I have great pleasure in offering two more books – 1. The Fourth Monkey and 2. Anjie, Pat and India's Poor, both under the banner of Notion Press, Chennai. I propose to publish a few more books from my stock of short stories from LiteraryVibes, the monthly eMagazine I edit.

I am grateful to the many writers and readers of LiteraryVibes who encouraged me by giving a positive feedback on my writing. I want to thank the many readers who conveyed their appreciation for the stories in my first two books. My wife Geetanjali, son Anuraag and his wife Kavitha; daughter Ankita and her husband Vivek; and our grandkids

- Shrey and Smyan have been my constant supporters. My writings are, in a way, a tribute to their love for me. A million thanks to them.

In continuation of my pledge last year I will gift a few copies of the two new books to those Old Age Homes, Hospitals, Public Libraries and Educational Institutions who were kind enough to acknowledge the receipt of The Jasmine Girl at Haji Ali and A Train to Kolkata sent to them.

So here I am, dear readers, dedicating to you my present book - Anjie, Pat and India's Poor - to read and pass your verdict. I will be grateful for your feedback at mrutyunjays@gmail.com or in my WhatsApp number +91-9930739537. If you like the stories please recommend the book to all your friends and contacts.

Mrutyunjay Sarangi

ANJIE, PAT AND INDIA'S POOR

Pat pushed a hot cauliflower pakoda into his mouth and blurted out,

"We have to take a quick decision. Can't wait anymore!"

The next moment his face darkened, sweat appeared on his forehead and he opened his mouth to emit smoke like a steam engine. The pakoda was obviously hot and my American citizen friend, unused to steaming pakodas, had misjudged its impact. He cried out, like a man surprised by a stinging scorpion,

"Holy shit! Why didn't you warn me how hot this goddamn stuff is?"

Since it was addressed to no one in particular, his wife Anjie laughed her head off,

"Serves you right, you incorrigible glutton, the moment you land in India you start filling your tummy with food. As if I don't give you any food back home. All this fried pakoda will keep you awake tonight, your poor tummy filled with gas like a freaking balloon!"

Pratap, my old classmate from high school, who had magically transformed into Pat in the U.S., whimpered;

his mouth stuffed with the third piece of pakoda consumed with a swiftness which would have given a kicking mule an inferiority complex,

"O, O, it is worth every ton of gas in the tummy, this heavenly stuff! And talking about the food you give me in America, let me tell you, even the prisoners in our jails in India get better stuff - at least they get freshly made rotis and sabji - not the grub prepared on Sundays, taken out of the freezer and heated up on rest of the days."

It was obvious to experienced eyes that a storm was appearing on their domestic horizon and before things went out of control my wife Kadambari dragged Anjana - Anjie to her friends and colleagues in America - to the kitchen to bring a plate of hot chicken pakodas which she knew would disappear in no time to make space for aloo pakodas as worthy successors in a grand lineage of the glorious pakoda clan.

Anjie and Pat, successful doctors in the U.S., had arrived from abroad in the early morning and checked in at Hotel Radisson near the Delhi airport. They usually did it every year on their annual trip to India. After checking in at the Radisson they would head straight for our government bungalow at Shahjahan Road and spend the whole day with us, catching up on all the gossip and stuffing themselves with the choicest dishes made by Kadamabari. Since I was indifferent to food and our son and daughter were away in their hostels, Kadambari used to prepare food fit for a royal feast for Anjie and Pat - dosa, idly, halwa for breakfast, chicken biriyani, fish fry and prawn curry for lunch and all kinds of assorted pakodas for the evening snacks. Dinner would be a 'light' affair with only mutton raganjosh and keema paratha. Pratap had an astonishingly gargantuan appetite and would do justice to all the dishes, sometimes openly and shamelessly licking his fingers, to squeals of laughter from Anjie, liberally sprinkled with endearing expletives. But Pat never cared and always ate with a gusto that bordered on exhibitionism. Obviously, both being doctors, they knew how to take care of rumbling tummies. They regretfully missed Kadambari's cooking on their return trip to U.S., preferring to go directly to the International Airport from the domestic one.

The first time Pat came to visit us around six years back, he took a long post-lunch nap and after getting up, gestured to Anjie to give him something. Anjie promptly handed over to him a roll of toilet paper from her bulging bag. Pat looked at me in embarrassment and murmured "Sorry, a dirty American habit" and ambled on to the toilet. Next year when he called to announce his impending trip I asked him not to bring toilet paper or mineral water from the US and promised to store them up before their arrival. Anjie and Pat never brought their two sons with them because on their first and only visit the kids had got frequent attacks of amoebiasis and copious mosquito bites had made their brown skin red.

Two years back, while munching on some puffed rice with mixture, Pat suddenly exclaimed,

"Satish, what's happening to this bloody country? Why is it deteriorating so fast?"

Curious, I asked him what happened.

"See, every time we land up at Delhi airport I hand over a bag containing a bottle of Black Label whisky and a carton of Marlboro cigarettes to the Customs official at the gate as a 'gift' and he lets us go. Yesterday even after I handed over the bag, someone else appeared, and asked me to open our two bags. He appeared to be the boss of the man who had taken the 'gift'. One look at him and I knew he meant trouble, so I took him aside, opened my wallet and told him, opening the bags is the same as opening the wallet. He took the wallet from me, extracted two hundred dollar bills and handed it back to me. When we left, you should have seen the way they saluted us, as if I was the President of India and had just signed their promotion order! Why Satish, why are they so unreasonable? Corruption within some norms is fine, but such open greed! Why this country is so wretched?"

I asked him why he had paid the bribe, was he carrying gold biscuits or some contraband?

Pat shook his head,

"Arey nehin yaar, no gold biscuit fiscuit, just a Nikon camera for my brother-in-law, a few watches for the nephews and nieces, some perfume and chocolates. The total worth may not be more than seven or eight hundred dollars. But after a twenty two hours journey who has the patience to go through a check by the Customs officials? And some of my friends have told me that once they open the bags, they will take out everything and take special pleasure in displaying your under garments to the wide eyed audience waiting in line."

We started laughing at this comic picture, but I continued,

"Why do you bring all this stuff with you, when everything is available in India?"

This time Anjie interjected,

"Everything is available here but the relatives want to show off the acquisitions from abroad. My Bhabhi takes special pleasure in giving away some chocolates to the lesser mortals with a warning 'to keep them in deep freezer, otherwise they will melt, having come from snowy climates like the U.S.'"

We had another round of laughter but Pat's frustration at the "deteriorating human values" continued to simmer within him. Like an obtuse Chinese philosopher he made a grand statement,

"Even if you are corrupt, maintain honesty in your dishonesty. If you lose your robe, heat and cold both are same for you."

That was two years ago. This time after the second cup of evening tea both Pat and Anjie expressed their rising sorrow over the growing poverty in India, and the falling standards of our roads and infrastructure. They had recently read somewhere about some starvation deaths in Odisha and their heart had melted like butter on a hot plate. They wanted to donate money for what they called the alleviation of poverty. Out of curiosity I asked them what was the amount they had in mind. Pat was about to say something, Anjie cut him short,

"Look Satish, money has no meaning for us. Both of us are well settled as doctors, our combined income is more than one million dollars per year. Both our sons are in Medical school and we have kept four hundred thousand for each of them in their bank account to cover their tuition fees and living expenses for the next five years. With a mansion in Chicago, a beach house in Tampa, Florida, a ranch in Texas and couple of apartments in La Jolla, San Diego, we don't need any more money. So we can spare about five thousand dollars a year for our poor countrymen."

I made a quick calculation. Five thousand dollars translated to something like three lakh rupees. What big change in poverty did Anjie and Pat want to make with this amount? But I waited to hear about their plan. Pat looked at me pointedly,

"Satish, why don't YOU do something for the poor? I can write a cheque to you for five thousand dollars now itself. Don't you feel for our poor?"

"Yes, of course I am pained by the widespread poverty in India, but I don't want to take your money. For the five thousand dollars you give me you will ask me fifty questions and keep on pestering me to know how I spent the money and how much poverty has been reduced by your kind gesture. I don't want that headache".

Pat exploded,

"See, see, this is the problem with you Indians! You don't want to act, just sit on your fat bottoms and give lectures!"

I couldn't contain my laughter,

"Hey Pratap, what do you mean, 'you Indians'? Since when have you ceased to be an Indian?"

Pat looked at me, embarrassed, and said,

"Sorry, just a slip of tongue! But tell me how to use our five thousand dollars for India's poor. They need it, you know."

"Give it to the Prime Minister's Relief Fund. It will be used to help the poor at the time of some natural disaster."

Pat shook his head in total disapproval,

"No! Why should we wait for a natural disaster for our money to be used for the poor? And we wouldn't know for whom the money has been used or for what. Tell me some other constructive way to do that"

I thought for a few seconds.

"Why not give it to some orphanage or Old Age Home?"

Pat looked at me angrily,

"You idiot, can't you think of some good use for our hard earned money? You want it to go for children or old people? With children we will have to wait for decades to see if someone who got the benefit of our money did anything meaningful in life. And with old people......."

Pat just wrinkled his nose, shook his head, and kept quiet.

I offered another suggestion,

"Give it to our school, you know the Salepur High School where you and I had studied? Ask the head master to buy a few computers and other modern equipment for the students."

Pat sat there for a few seconds, with his head bent in some kind of a silent despair.

"Five years back I had sent two thousand dollars to my uncle to hand over to the head master of our old school to construct a new modern laboratory for the students. You know what happened? My uncle told me that the head master had got the dollars converted to rupees and kept it at home. His son, a good for nothing scoundrel, somehow came to know that more than a lakh rupees was kept at home. He beat up his father and ran away with the money to Kolkata with a couple of friends and returned after a fortnight, all the money spent on liquor and whores. I don't want to waste my money again with those useless people."

I tried to persuade him,

"You don't have to give to the Head Master, just give the money to the BDO of Salepur Block, he will get the work done and give the completion certificate to you."

Anjana cut me short and exploded,

"BDO? You mean Block Development Officer? My God, BDOs are the most corrupt people in government. One of my uncles was a BDO. One day his house was raided and the police got papers for property worth ninety lakh rupees, seven lakh rupees cash, jewelry worth twenty lakhs, all made from loot of public money. We don't want to touch a BDO even with a barge pole."

Anjana was so emphatic that I suggested they donate the money to an NGO.

Pat made a big face as if he had just swallowed a baby python instead of an aloo pakoda,

"Brother! NGOs are pure poison. One of my friends in Philly gave a few thousand dollars to an NGO in his home state of Bihar. Later, it came out the NGO was a fraud and had no authorization to collect funds from abroad. An enquiry was ordered and some government officials made repeated trips to the U.S. and other countries to conduct the enquiry. I am sure with their frequent jaunts they spent more money than the amount involved in fraud. My friend was summoned by the Embassy fellows three times and had to go to Washington to attend the enquiry. I don't want to get into that kind of a mess."

That put me in a fix. I thought I had exhausted all options; suddenly my eyes were drawn to Kadambari. Poor thing, she was tired after a day's hard work and had dozed off on a chair. Looking at her I had an inspiration! Women's empowerment! Yes, we had to empower women, we had to awaken the sleeping lot, and make them a part of India's growth story. I snapped my fingers and announced triumphantly,

"Pratap, your problem is solved. Women's empowerment! We will spend that money on women's empowerment. It's a worthy cause and nothing is worthier than that. Moreover in India anything that has to do something with women draws attention like half-clad devotees to a non-clad Baba."

Anjie and Pat sat up, instantly electrified and shouted,

"Yes, you have hit the nail on the head. Our money will fly like a magic carpet carrying women to dizzying heights! Wow, such an exciting idea! But tell me how to spend it on this worthy cause?"

I shared their enthusiasm like a schoolboy returning home after winning a trophy, and blurted out,

"There are so many NGOs working for women's empowerment. We can work through them".

Next moment I jumped up as if a bomb had exploded under my chair, Pat shouted like an agitated headmaster disciplining a wayward student,

"NGO? Again NGO? Didn't I tell you we just don't trust those blighters? Why do you want us to get into trouble, just because we want to do something for our poor country?"

I was a little embarrassed, like an innocent schoolboy who was being scolded by his teacher for unwittingly wetting his pants. Even Kadambari woke up from her dozing at Pat's shouting.

Before I could say anything more, the doorbell rang. It was the taxi driver who had come to ask if there would be more delay and if he could go and finish his dinner somewhere. Anjie was annoyed. They had engaged the taxi for the whole day, hadn't they? So why was the idiot asking this stupid question? She was unusually aggressive,

"Yes, we will be here till eleven. You have some problem with that?"

The driver was taken by surprise by her harshness,

"No Memsaab, If you are going to be late I will go and have dinner in some dhaba nearby."

Anjie shouted at him,

"So? Go and have your grub and come, why are you asking for permission?"

The driver smiled obsequiously and kept standing there. Pat went to the door, took out two hundred rupees from his pocket and gave it to him and asked him to return by ten. The driver saluted him and went away. Anjie exploded like a Diwali bomb, and snapped at Pat,

"You gave him two hundred rupees? Two freaking hundred? Look at the bloody swine, we pay him four thousand rupees for the day's hire and he expects money for dinner? Why can't he spend his own money for his grub?"

I was speechless! These two earned an income of one million dollars a year. And cribbing for tips of two hundred rupees which was less than three and half dollars! I couldn't restrain myself,

"But Anjie, in U.S. you must be tipping the taxi drivers, the waitresses in restaurants? And that would be at least ten dollars? So why do you mind paying two hundred rupees to the taxi driver here?"

Anjie shot back, like a cobra spitting venom,

"Come on Satish, is there any comparison? America is America, the richest country in the world! But India is so cheap, everything is so cheap here! You don't need two hundred rupees to have a meal here! This idiot Pat is so freaking gullible! God knows what comes over him when he lands in India; he over-tips everyone, forgetting that this is such a cheap place!"

I winced, as if hit by cruel shots from a gun. A great sadness enveloped my being like a dark cloud covering the sky. Cheap? My country may be poor, but certainly not cheap! The poor in my country suffered as much from hunger and pain as the poor anywhere in the world, including America. Hunger had no nationality, no colour, no religion. It was expressed in only one language - the language of pain and of a miserable frustration at an uncaring God who kept people hungry. My people in India felt the same sorrow at a relative's death, their heart breaking into thousands of twisted pieces as anyone in a rich country like the U.S. If a nail bit the feet it caused the same amount of pain everywhere in the world, making people cry! There was nothing cheap about hunger, pain, tears! How heartless of Anjana to say India was a cheap country!

Kadambari could sense my sadness; she invited all of us to dinner and over food asked Pat,

"So, how are you going to empower the women?"

Pat smiled,

"Forget it, I can't go from town to town with a bagful of dollars and tell women, 'Come, come, I will empower you!' It will be like a barber going around with a razor calling men to come to him so that he can shave their beard!"

The comparison was so outlandish that we all burst out laughing. Anjie took a big chunk of the keema paratha, dipped it in Raganjosh and moved by the heavenly taste, looked admiringly at Kadambari,

"Look Kadambari, the only way out is to hand over the five thousand dollars to you to spend on some worthwhile cause. I am sure you as a woman will understand poverty better than thick-headed men!"

Kadambari liked the idea, particularly her superiority over thick-headed men. She jumped at the proposal like a child grabbing a handful of lollipops,

"Yes, give me the money; I will buy blankets for the poor and the homeless during winter which is just two months away. So many of them sleep under the flyovers and keep shivering through winter nights, some of them even die, unable to withstand the severe cold!"

Anjana sat up as if she had just swallowed a frog which had accidentally strayed into the Raganjosh. And like Katrina Kaif in the song Sheela Ki Jawani she said in a singsong voice,

"No no no no, no no no no; don't do that. No no, I won't allow that. I had read somewhere that these buggers sell off the blankets for a hundred rupees or so and spend the money on buying drugs or charas. We don't want our hard earned dollars to go up in charas smoke!"

With that I felt we had reached a stalemate. We had been discussing this subject for more than two hours and had reached nowhere, after traversing in all directions. We finished dinner and over a dessert of rasmalai I suggested to Pat that he should find a good, deserving institution like CARE or Oxfam International and donate his five thousand dollars to them. Anjie and Pat gathered their things and started walking towards the taxi. I opened the door for them. Pat turned to me and with deep hurt in his voice, said,

"Satish, how could you even think of such a ghastly thing? Hard earned money of Anjie and mine will go to institutions outside India? Why, are the poor in India so unfortunate? They won't get a penny of our charity? Please, don't speak like that, my brother. We are prepared to wait for one more year. Meanwhile, locate good recipients for our money. When we come next year we will finalise."

With that assurance they left. I turned, my heart weighed down by an indefinable sadness. I murmured to myself, "Pat and Anjie, you will go back to the U.S. after two weeks and get busy earning your million dollars and planning to buy another beach house in San Francisco or a ranch in Colorado. Till you come on your trip next year, India will add one more million people to its poor, the rich will get richer, the hungry hungrier. Our pompous and overfed leaders will give a thousand more heart-wrenching speeches on poverty and hunger in the legislatures. But within the next one year how do I locate deserving individuals, selfless NGOs or honest leaders for your donation of five thousand dollars?"

GLOSSARY

Arey nehin yaar – No, my friend

BDO – Block Development Officer

Charas – Cannabis

Dhaba – Roadside eatery

Keema – Minced meat

Memsaab – Madam

Pakoda, dosa, idly, halwa, biriyani, roti, paratha, sabji – Delicious items of snacks and food

Ragan josh – Delicious mutton preparation in Kashmiri style

Rasmalai – A popular dessert made of milk, cottage cheese and sugar

– 2 –

HAPPY BIRTHDAY

The small girl came to Neel at the party and said, "When will I have my birthday party"?

He asked, "Why do you want a party"?

She smiled sweetly at him, "So that I will get a lot of gifts".

He told her "Come with me, I will buy you lots of toys and dresses". She again smiled, "But uncle, I also want a cake, candles and balloons". He promised her all that. But then, she walked away dismissing the whole idea, "Nah, I also want a crowd to sing Happy Birthday to me! You seem to be so alone"!

The man looked wistfully at the receding figure of the cute little girl. Ah, such a pretty child! It is as if God had made her in his own image - beautiful, innocent and playful!

Neel looked across the hall, to the other end where the ladies were chatting. His guess was right. Madhu was looking at him. She had seen the girl approaching him and then walking away. Her face was sad and she was shaking her head in a very subtle way which only her husband could decipher.

She knew, as he did, the emptiness in their heart when it pined for a child, cried for peals of laughter in the house, for toys strewn on the floor, the incessant demand for munchies, pastries, and ice cream. The rosy cheeks, the curly hair, the hunt for cosmetics in Mom's closet, the endless fight with Neel for candies - all this and much more were missing from their lives.

This is what Madhu's elder sister Anjali talked of incessantly, when she visited with her three daughters, all in their teens. They were a bunch of livewires, never sitting quiet, constantly picking up fights with each other. Madhu always cried silently for a few days after they left.

Neel knew he could not father a child with Madhu. The doctor had told them in no uncertain terms about his deficiency, the low sperm-count. Their little world had got devastated the day they heard the verdict. And by the time they reached home they had discussed so many possibilities.

The discussions had continued for days. Since Neel's low sperm-count was the problem they had decided to go for artificial fertilisation by getting sperm from a donor. The doctor had agreed to help them. They just wanted a few more days to decide.

And then the new maid came. A young girl of around twenty five, Shanta was efficiency personified, doing her work in a silent, professional way. Yet, one look at her and there was no mistaking the shadow of sadness hovering over her all the time. It took just one week for Madhu to win her confidence; she had a way of dealing with people which endeared her to them. Shanta poured her heart out to Madhu on the tenth day. Yes, she was sad, carrying a devastation of her life on her young shoulders. She had lost a two years old child just six months back. It was a baby girl, so beautiful that Shanta used to put an extra dot of kajal on her forehead to ward off all evil. Yet that could not save her.

Madhu was sympathetic, consoled the crying girl and asked her what happened. Shanta told a story which would melt the stoniest of the hearts. Shanta had married Lalit at sixteen, as was usual in their community. They were childless for five years and then it was found that Lalit had a kamjori, a deficiency which prevented conceiving of a child. The doctor suggested artificial fertilisation by getting sperm from a donor. Lalit agreed, but very reluctantly, and the child was born, the prettiest girl in their basti. Shanta was delirious with joy, they named her Meena. Lalit's celebration was muted. He would often look at the child in a strange way, as if he was trying to know who she resembled, who was her father. Shanta knew that Lalit never accepted her as his daughter but looking at Meena's face she didn't care.

And one day when she had gone out to attend to her work, leaving Meena in Lalit's charge, her darling daughter died mysteriously. Lalit could never explain how she died, except that she was sleeping after food and didn't wake up. Shanta knew he had killed her by giving her some poison. Shanta kept sobbing, "A man will never allow his wife to carry another person's child Madam, he will burn with jealousy and his ego will be shattered. If I knew Lalit would not accept Meena I would not have brought her to the world Madam. God will never forgive me."

Madhu of course knew an educated man like Neel would be different from Lalit. But a slight doubt had seeped into the mind and lingered there. The idea got shelved.

Neel was immersed in thoughts. He woke up from his reveries when someone tugged at his hand. He looked down. The same cute little girl smiled and said, come Uncle, the birthday girl is waiting to cut the cake. Neel walked in a daze, looking at the sweet face of the little girl. A crowd was gathering around the table in the centre of the hall.

Madhu was standing a little distance away talking to two ladies; the dark clouds in her heart were covered by a plastic smile on the face. Neel wanted to lift the cute little child so that she can see the cake cutting directly. But she had left. Neel felt crestfallen. His eyes kept searching for her. And then he found the little angel guiding one more uncle to the centre of the hall. Neel sighed. His heart ached and cried out for a little angel he never had. And he felt so alone!

GLOSSARY

Basti – A colony, usually of economically backward people

Kajal – Kohl (Collyrium) applied on the eyes for enhancing beauty. A small dot of Kajal is also applied on the forehead of small children to ward off evil

3

FRAGRANCE

The telephone kept ringing. Surajit rushed from the balcony and picked it up. There was a lady on the other side.

"Hello, did I wake you up? What is the time there? Can you guess who this is? I bet you can't!"

Surajit was puzzled. Who could it be? He hardly got calls from ladies. A couple of old, fat Gujarati clients tried a few times to call him at home; he stopped it by telling them curtly that he took business calls only at office. And this caller sounded much younger. Wait a second, she asked what time was it here. Someone from abroad?

"Sorry, not able to place you. Who are you? You are asking about the time here? Where are you calling from? America? Australia? Antarctica?"

The lady at the other end chuckled,

"I knew you would answer my questions with your counter questions. Your old habit, of more than thirty years, remember? You were hardly thirteen at the time. How time flies! Difficult to imagine we were once upon a time kids, throwing questions and trying to outsmart each other!"

Surajit got a shock. Thirty years back? Was this Sunayana? My God, she has not lost any of the zing in her voice, the same liveliness, full of animation and effervescence! Surajit's mind filled with a warmth, a glow. A mild euphoria washed over him. He was startled by the booming voice on the other side, floating over blue oceans and across the wide skies,

"Hello, where are you lost? I know you have guessed who I am. And like the Surajit of the past you must have been seized by a glow of gentle love. Always the shy, sentimental boy. I knew you were a gone case, even thirty years back!"

Surajit smiled,

"Yes, a gone case, perhaps that's why you never wrote a letter to me from Jamshedpur after you left Cuttack!"

Sunayana laughed,

"Are you crazy? How could I write to you? Those days I even didn't know where the post office was, and if I wanted to write to you, I would have to give the letter to Daddy to drop in the letter box. You think my Daddy would have liked it? And you know, two years after we returned to Jamshedpur Daddy came over to the U.S., did his Ph.D., got a job and we settled down here. Tell me, did you ever remember me all these years?"

Surajit wanted to tell her, he didn't remember her often, but he hadn't forgotten her, or the one week of happy adolescence they had spent together in the summer of 1972 at his home in Buxi Bazar, Cuttack. Instead, he threw the question back at her,

"Did you? Did I ever come to your mind after you left Cuttack thirty years back?"

Sunayana hesitated,

"I don't want to lie to you. I had missed you a lot after I returned from Cuttack. I often felt like telling my parents to go to Cuttack so that I could see you again, but I felt too shy to do that. Once we came to the U.S. I got busy; new place, new friends, and time just flew. I got married. My husband Saurav is a nuclear scientist, very quiet, dignified and caring. I have not been to India for the past seven years. Busy with our only son, his studies, his games and extracurricular activities. But I had never forgotten you. And last week when we decided to visit India, I felt I must meet you. I don't know why you came to my mind again and again, like a never-forgotten sweet old song. I spoke to uncle, getting his number from my dad. He had attended my wedding; you were in Mumbai at the time. I got your number from him and here I am talking to you! But see, like the old days, I do all the talking and you do the listening, the quiet, bashful prince listening to a lesser mortal!"

Surajit felt a thrill go through him like a mild current again, being called a quiet, bashful prince. That was what Sunayana used to call him!

"Is your son coming with you?"

"No, he just got into Medical school in Chicago. Can't take time off. Saurav has some meetings at Bhabha Atomic Research Center; they had offered accommodation at their guest house. I told Saurav we would stay with you. For three days, from January sixth to ninth. Tell Vandana to keep herself free, she and I will go shopping all the three days."

Surajit smiled,

"So you have found out my wife's name! What else do you know about me?"

"Uncle was so happy talking about you! He thinks you are the best son-husband-father in the world. There is so much pride in him for you! I am impressed. You must be awesome!"

"Was I not awesome when you saw me? Thirty years back?"

"No, I was the one who was awesome, defeating you in every game, even in arm wrestling! But you were awesome to be with. Okay, time to stop. We will talk about all that when I come there."

Surajit panicked,

"Listen, I have not told Vandana about you. She doesn't know that you ever came into my life, although it was just for a week. Please don't say anything that will embarrass me."

Sunayana laughed,

"Don't worry; I am not coming to rock your happy family boat. Our account has been settled thirty years back, with what you gave me and what you took from me. Don't you remember?"

Sunayana chuckled and put down the phone.

Surajit walked to the window and looked out. From his twelfth floor apartment at Malabar Hills the Arabian Sea looked calm and blue. He had an hour to himself. Vandana would be busy with her Pooja till nine thirty. The maid had left, after cooking breakfast and lunch. Anup and Sulagna had left for school. He smiled to himself. How did everything change in a few minutes? With just a phone call from a long lost friend from the past who had briefly appeared in his life as a twelve year old girl and left with a memory so fragrant, so intoxicating that after all these years Surajit felt a mild glow spreading over his consciousness like the smell of musk overpowering his senses! He smiled, remembering her parting words a few moments back! Remember her? How could Surajit forget that wonderful one week they had spent in his Buxi Bazar home at Cuttack in a hot summer of adolescence?

Till the summer of 1972 Surajit didn't know what it meant talking to a girl, sitting near her, holding her hand and the next minute fighting with her over meaningless issues. All that changed in the summer vacation that year when his father announced that his close friend Ghanashyam uncle was coming to visit them for a week along with Auntie and Sunayana, their thirteen year old daughter. Surajit was happy. Sunayana! What a lovely name! And she was the same age as he; they would chat a lot about their school and their friends. How would she be? Would her eyes be as beautiful as her name suggested? He was happy with a suppressed excitement. Finally the day of their arrival came. He accompanied his father to the railway station to receive them. His Maa stayed back at home to prepare food for the guests.

When Surajit saw Sunayana for the first time, he smiled to himself. How did this lanky, darkish girl, who looked like a skeleton with a dash of flesh here and there, a lock of unruly hair falling over her face, stir his imagination these past four days? But, my God! She was so tall! She reminded him of the picture of a beautiful horse standing tall and proud on a calendar they had at home. He touched the feet of uncle and aunty and shyly smiled at her. She looked at him pointedly, absolutely devilish in her grin,

"My name is Sunayana. Don't try to call me Nayana or something like that. I hate that."

Her mother tried to shush her,

"Stop it; don't talk like that to him! Didn't I tell you he is a brilliant student, always tops his class, not an ignorant monkey like you?"

Sunayana looked away and the moment her mother moved with a bag to where the two old friends were standing, she looked at him, stuck out her tongue and made a big face at him, trying her best to imitate a monkey. Surajit had never seen a girl make a face at him and had always thought it must be a dirty gesture. But for a moment he was stunned, captivated by the utterly girlish beauty of the act.

They had to hire two cycle rickshaws. His father and uncle took one rickshaw keeping all the luggage and Aunty sat in the second one with the two kids on either side. She was visiting Cuttack after many years and was trying to check how much the town had changed. Sunayana took over the social nicety of a conversation. In no time she found out which class was Surajit in, how many friends he had, what games he played, how much he scored in maths and half a dozen other bits of information. Then suddenly, as if by an inspiration, she asked her mother,

"Mama, the shirt we have brought for Surajit, don't you think it will be a little tight for him? He looks like a mini buffalo, doesn't he? My God, how many eggs does he eat every day? Four? Six? And what kind of egg, hen's egg or duck's egg?"

Her mother was scandalised and shouted at Sunayana,

"Hey monkey, what sort of question is that? You think everyone is like you? Eat like a cow and grow like a monkey?

All skin and bones? Be careful, don't fight with Surajit! One slap from him and you will be flattened to the ground!"

Sunayana clapped, "See, you also agree that he is fat, like a Sumo wrestler!"

Surajit's face coloured at this insult and Sunayana got a slap from her mother with a warning to keep quiet. Surajit looked straight; Sunayana extended her hand behind her mother and pinched him on his right arm. When he looked at her, she put out her tongue and made a big face at him, putting her hands on her ears and blowing up her cheeks trying to look like a wrestler!

After they reached home and had their breakfast, Sunayana and her parents had a bath. When she came out to the sitting room with a yellow frock and a red ribbon, her hair nicely plaited, Surajit's heart skipped a beat. What had appeared to be a darkish complexion due to the dust and soot of the fourteen hours of train journey was gone and Sunayana looked quite beautiful. Surajit felt her presence near him, she was pulling him to go out and pluck mangoes from the tree in the garden. They went out. The heat was unbearable; they sat in the shade of the tree. Away from the gaze of the parents Sunayana was unstoppable, she kept chatting about her school (boring in studies, but exciting in sports), her friends (almost everyone in the class was a friend, appan kisise dartaa nehin, I am not scared of anyone, can beat the daylights out of anybody), her likes and dislikes in food (pickles are my favourite, ah, the varieties of pickles you get outside the school! But I hate non-veg food, smells too much!), songs (dance walla song, not the ronaa dhonaa type), movies (only action movies, when the heroine beats up someone I stand up and cheer! Don't like the romantic somantic film, too painful, appanko hansnaa maangtaa hai, ronaa nehin!). She was an endless chatterer and Surajit an obedient listener, looking at her face, the beautiful face with smiles constantly breaking like waves in the ocean, the sparkling eyes full of mischief and the soft hair blowing in the mild summer wind. He had hardly spoken when she asked,

"How are your friends, all quiet like you, or you have someone like my type also, chatting all the time?"

Surajit tried to remember who among his friends was the non-stop chattering type, he remembered nobody. He asked her back, "Are all your friends like you?"

She laughed, "O, question to counter a question? That's your style? No, I have all types of friends. Bharati is a big actress, you should see the way her face changes expressions when she talks, as if she is trying to impress you all the time. And Santoshini? She is the champion crier, when the school closes for vacation she cries, going from friend to friend and telling them she would miss them and when the school reopens she cries because she had missed everyone! Before an exam starts she cries out of fear, after the exam ends she cries out of relief!"

Surajit asked her,

"How about you, are you not scared of exams?"

Sunayana laughed, like a waterfall cascading,

"Aapan? Aapan exam se nehin dartaa hai! Why should I be scared? I know I won't score more than fifty percent in any subject. But in sports I am the champion, no one can beat me in any form of running, long jump and triple jump. I get so many cups that my dad has to bring a bag to carry them home after the annual sports meet."

Surajit tried to tease her,

"But how can you be good in running? You look like a skeleton!"

"So what? I run like a skeleton also, long steps, no one can catch up with me."

She kept quiet for a moment, and continued,

"You can beat me in maths, or science, but you can't match me in talking, in running or jumping"

"And in making faces? How many types of faces can you make?"

"O, all types, at least twenty types; want to see?"

"No, not now. Let's go inside, lunch must be ready."

That's how they went on and on. Surajit's father and uncle used to leave home after breakfast to meet their college friends. The mothers used to be chatting all the time, going for shopping in the evening. Surajit and Sunayana were inseparable, like two long-lost friends who had found each other after years. Sunayana would play all kinds of pranks on him,

"Tell me O ignorant prince, why am I called Sunayana? Are my eyes beautiful? Or are you reluctant to answer this innocent question, my quiet and bashful prince?"

The usually serious Surajit would try to make a face,

"Nothing about you is beautiful, you lady skeleton! You are too skinny".

Sunayana would explode in mock anger and start beating him up. For a skinny girl, she was surprisingly strong. Surajit would never think of raising his hand against her, not even once.

They would play Ludo, carrom and cards; Sunayana would always make it a point to win. Surajit would never mind losing to this cracker of a girl. A new-found joy in losing innocent games kept him in a dreamlike state all the time. In the evenings they would go to the nearby market and drink lassi. On the way back they would stop at the Amareswar temple and look at the toys and trinkets in the small shops outside the gate.

When night came and it was time to sleep, Surajit's heart would break into inconsolable pieces. He would miss Sunayana's chatter, her pranks, her mild rebukes and the words of endearment like O Silent Stone, My Shy Prince, O Bashful Genius and all that. The thought of separation from her for a few hours in the night would make him sad, he wished they wouldn't have to be separated even for that little time and after the lights were switched off he would bury his face in the pillow and shed silent tears.

The one week passed like a dream. On the day before the departure Surajit and Sunayana went to the market, had the famous thunka puri and currry from the Buxi Bazar market, and took lassi from their usual shop. They stopped outside the temple and Surajit bought a beautiful, colourful wooden bird and gifted it to Sunayana. For a moment he looked deep into her eyes, and said, "This is for remembrance, whenever you see this bird, you will remember me, won't you?" Sunayana only nodded her head and looked away.On the way home she challenged him to have a race. He couldn't catch up with her. She made a face at him and said "You can't beat me in anything, except of course, studies. In that Aapan is a zero."

Surajit looked at her and said,

"I can certainly beat you in arm wrestling. My arm is four times heavier than yours".

She shook her head,

"No way, even there also I will beat you hands down," and she gestured how she would do it.

When they reached home their mothers were waiting for them. They had to go to the neighbour's house so that Sunayana's mother could take leave of the Aunty there. Their train was at nine in the morning the next day. The moment Surajit and Sunayana entered the living room they squatted on the ground and started arm wrestling. Although Surajit was heavier, he had no idea about the lanky girl's strength. Within a minute she was pinning his hand down. Surajit was not prepared to accept defeat, he tickled her on the waist with his left hand and in a moment her grip loosened and he could bend her hand to the ground. She was furious! She started shouting at him, Cheat; you cheat, and started tickling him. In no time they were wrestling with each other in a mock fight. Soon he was lying flat on the floor and she had climbed over him, sitting on his chest and tickling him.

In a few moments a new, hitherto-unknown sensation flooded over Surajit. He looked at her, his eyes dazed and sweats glistening on his face. He felt as if the person sitting on his body was not a mere bundle of bones and flesh, but something far from physical; she was an embodiment of lyrical love and liquid longing, petals of flowers taking the shape of the most exquisite body God has made, emitting a fragrance of immortal beauty. He looked at her helplessly, his hands lying by his sides. The game had stopped and a new chapter of life had suddenly opened up for them. She looked at him, blushed a deep red and ran away to her mother in the neighbour's house.

The rest of the evening was spent on marveling over the new flame of love that had awakened in Surajit and Sunayana, as if they had crossed a barrier and come of age. They looked at each other, but there was no more a desire to play any games. Surajit wanted to give himself away to her, losing every game they played, only if she could stay back with him. She had no desire left for winning any game with Surajit. It was as if the summer wind was blowing across a meadow of scented flowers and whispering in her ears the message of a youthful awakening in her, telling her she had just embarked on a wonderful journey where wins and losses would no longer have a meaning - the body, heart and soul would yearn to surrender themselves to a selfless love leading to a fathomless fulfillment.

Next morning there was hectic activity at home, in preparation for the departure to the railway station. Surajit and Sunayana could not look at each other: their eyes were brimming with tears. Surajit was sitting in his room, head bent over his knees, deep in sadness. Suddenly Sunayana stormed into the room,

"Have you seen my yellow frock, I have looked for it everywhere and cannot find it."

Surajit looked up, his face clouded with an injured innocence,

"No, how would I know about your frock? The yellow one? In which you look like a blooming sunflower?"

She nodded and proceeded to open the only cupboard in the room. Surajit shouted,

"Please don't open that cupboard. It has only my clothes and books."

Sunayana had already opened it and there, under Surajit's shirts was the yellow frock, obviously taken by Surajit from the clothes drying in the courtyard and hidden there. Sunayana was furious! She wanted to shout at him, to call him a thief. But a look at his sad, melancholic face and she realised something had changed in them on the previous evening and they had entered a world which was beyond a small act of losing or finding a frock. It was a world of hearts and souls washed in an ethereal fragrance of love. She looked at Surajit's tear-streaked face, the eyes appealing to her to leave something of her with him. She quietly replaced the frock under the shirts in the cupboard and left the room, her head bowed, eyes brimming with tears.

Surajit's mother came to call him one final time to come with them to the station but he shook his head and stayed back at home on the pretext of a headache. He went out and touched the feet of Uncle and Aunty and took their blessings. He and Sunayana didn't look at each other. The separation was breaking their hearts; they didn't want to show the fragments to their parents.

Surajit never heard from Sunayana again, nor did he try to write to her. The quiet, bashful prince remained imprisoned in his own image, afraid to let out his secret to his parents. His Maa however found the frock after a few months while arranging the clothes in his cupboard. She was surprised to see it there. She took it to Surajit,

"Arey Kunu, I found this frock in your cupboard. Did Sunayana leave it there by mistake? Let me give it to your Baba, he will send it to Jamshedpur through someone from his office."

Surajit looked at his Maa, a sad pain crowding his face. His mother was surprised again, at this tragic innocence. She looked at him, smiled indulgently and said, "My innocent child, when will you grow up?"

That was thirty years back. Surajit knew his Maa would have kept the yellow frock in some trunk somewhere, its frail folds a remnant of an innocent boy's adolescent dream. Today Sunayana's call brought back all those memories and filled his heart with a soft undercurrent of joy, as if he had found some long lost object of sweet desire.

Sunayana came to Mumbai after a few days with her husband Saurav. Anup and Sulagna fell in love with this loud mouth Aunty from the moment of her arrival. She had found out from Surajit's father that Anup loved Nintendo games and Sulagna liked to collect Keyboards and played lovely music on them. They got these beautiful gifts from their American Aunty and Uncle. Saurav was busy with his conference. Vandana accompanied Sunayana for extensive shopping. Kebabs at Bade Miyan, Ice cream at Rustam's and loads of food to bring home - that was Sunayana. When they met in the evening there was endless chatter; Saurav and Surajit enjoying her banter. The house was filled with excitement and noise. Three days passed in a jiffy. On the morning they were getting ready to leave for the airport, Saurav had gone to the washroom. Sunayana was effusive in her praise of Vandana,

"You are such a nice darling Vandana! I don't have a sister, but if I had one she would not have done as much as you did for us. Last three days you have been running around in Mumbai City with me and taking care of us. I will never forget you. I am a big memory buff, I love my memories. Most of my precious memories have a unique fragrance of their own,"

Vandana cut her short,

"Fragrance? How can a memory have a fragrance?"

"Yes there are some memories, when they come they flood your consciousness with a rare fragrance, you can smell them like they happened just yesterday and have not stopped happening. Many years back a friend of mine had gifted me a colourful wooden bird. I have kept it with me and every time I look at it, I feel as if he is standing with me, looking into my eyes and saying 'This is for remembrance. Will you remember me, always?'"

Surajit felt a stab in his heart. He knew exactly who had said that. He looked at Sunayana, a cold appeal in his eyes. Sunayana had become pensive; she was looking at the wide open sea, the cool air undulating its surface with gentle waves. Saurav came out, all ready to leave. Surajit's heart started thumping; what if Vandana asked Sunayana who that friend was and what she had given him in exchange for the wooden bird?

In a trembling voice Surajit said, "You are getting late for the flight. Sorry I can't come down with you. Vandana will see you off. I am getting late for the office".

Surajit knew his heart was thumping so loudly that it would resound in the small lift, giving him away. He stayed back, waving at Sunayana. He remembered, thirty years back on a similar morning of farewell he could not go to the railway station to see her off. Ah, he said to himself, the fragrance of some memories! So intensely overpowering, so debilitatingly mesmerising!

GLOSSARY

Aapan – Me

Aapan exam se nehin dartaa hai – I am not scared of exams

Appanko hansnaa maangtaa hai, ronaa nehin – I like laughter, not crying

Lassi – Sweetened butter milk

Ronaa dhonaa – Crying

4

SOFT FOOTSTEPS

It was a pleasantly cool January morning in Cuttack. I woke up to an enchanting world of soft, smiling sunshine. Birds were twittering their happy songs with careless abandon and washed by the overnight dew, the flowers were radiant with a rare beauty. I felt like taking a long walk, down memory lane, right up to my old high school. After a leisurely breakfast I was getting ready to leave, when my elder brother called out,

"Where are you going? You arrived only last night, take some rest."

"It is so beautiful outside. Let me take a walk up to our old neighborhood and to my high school and see how much they have changed in the past eight years."

My brother was shocked.

"You want to walk all the way to the old school? It's more than three miles from here! Why don't you engage a rickshaw?"

My Bhabhi joined in a teasing banter,

"No, no, let him take a walk. In the U.S. he must be going by car everywhere. Here at least the soil of Cuttack town will be sanctified by the footprints of the American citizen!"

Coming out of my brother's home in Ranihat, I smiled and muttered to myself,

"You are wrong Bhabhi. It is not Cuttack's soil, but my own soul which will be sanctified by the sweet, loving touch of this beautiful town, the abode of my childhood, and the repository of millions of priceless memories."

Having roamed around the world and seen dozens of cities in the U.S., Europe and Asia, the place that still stirred the depth of my soul was this small town, teeming with a million people, bound by the rivers Mahanadi on one side and Kathjodi on the other. Every time I woke up to a foggy, winter morning anywhere, I remembered my childhood days, shivering hands thrust in the pockets, walking half asleep to the tuition teacher's house at the break of dawn. The street lights would be still on, creating a make-believe world of semi-light and semi-darkness.

On some afternoons in my office at the University of Texas, an eerie melancholy would jab me in the ribs, bringing the taste of sweet lassi from my favorite shop in Buxi Bazaar. Evenings on the Champs de Elysees in Paris would remind me of the walk down the main street of Cuttack, captivated by the colourful lights in the shops, dazzling the expansive corners of a young boy's mind.

Sitting on the banks of the river Volga with its dimly lighted promenade would take me back to the memory of river Mahanadi, and to the autumn mornings when we used to go to the Gadagadia Ghat to float small bamboo-stick boats, to commemorate the historic journey of a past generation of sailors to unknown islands of promised prosperity.

And the nights? Nights of Cuttack of the sixties were filled with the curiosity of a town welcoming new pastures of pleasure, the giant wheels, merry-go-rounds at the Barabati fair site, the restaurants, the movie halls and the circus. For children like us it was a voyage of discovery, holding the hands of the elders and walking down unknown territories with a new sense of awe and wonder. And the rare occasions when one could pass through the posh Cantonment Road under the canopy of the huge, gulmohar trees on a full moon night, drenched in the magical illusion of a hide-and-seek game of light and shadow! Ah, what divine, pristine beauty! One would never see it again, lost in the bright display of dazzling lights in our cities.

At my home in College Station, Texas, the shadow that would suddenly wake me up with a start in the dead of night, was the memory of the famed ghosts of Gora Kabar, the Whitemen's Cemetery in Cuttack. And the sound that would appear from nowhere and leave a painful echo in the mind, was the music of the small flute bought in the Baliyatra fair when I was in the second grade in school.

The winter afternoons in my childhood would be filled with the excitement of flying kites in the clear, blue sky. The kite fights, the defeat of the unknown rival, the crazy, breathless running after the dismembered kites, and the joy of grabbing one ahead of the others, as if a booty of gold had fallen into the hand! What innocent, inexpensive pleasure! Where would our children get it now, with their video games, Nintendos and Internet? How many times in my life my eyes had scanned the sky of Paris, Shanghai and Berlin in vain, waiting for a mere glimpse of a kite!

Flashes of memory ran through my mind, filling me with a rare joy and pure bliss. In the past eight years

I must have taken this walk in my mind a hundred times, trying to visualize every stone on the way, every tree and the unforgettable landmarks! This time I had come to my favorite town after a long gap of eight years. This trip to India was for a mere ten days, of which only two days were meant for Cuttack. When one came on a trip to India from the U.S., everything had to be planned, every hour accounted for. Even a slight disruption or deviation would upset the whole schedule, leading to tension!

I could feel how Cuttack had changed in the past eight years. So many new shops, so many cars and so much crowd! Yet, in the jingling bells of the bicycles, the shout of the street hawkers, in the bargaining banter of the shopkeepers, there was a flavour of familiarity, a nostalgia. And with it, came the assurance of the town, that no matter where you went, you still belonged to me, as I belonged to you. Cuttack was like a beloved who never aged, one whom ravages of time left untouched; it was the ever-green beauty that grew lovelier with every passing year, radiating with the smiling brightness of the sun during the day and drenched by the soft serenity of the moon in the night.

I just crossed Machhua bazaar. A few steps ahead would be the Patnaik Motors and at the next turn Manisahu Chhak, where we had spent so many summer nights watching street plays under the open sky. The minor excitement of fights for space, the dozing off during the plays and sudden waking up to find one's sandals stolen! The numerous cups of tea, the struggle to keep awake in the night, the deep sleep in the day and then getting ready again for another night of street plays! Ah! How blissful were those adolescent days!

There, at the corner of the Manisahu Chhak, I saw the famous street shop, whose owner used to claim that any time during the day if the shop was seen without a customer, he would give away all the snacks free for that day. The variety of snacks at his shop was incredible! And what unbelievable, out-of-the-world taste! The sizzling baraa, aloochap, pakudi, goolgula, baigini, and piaji coming out of the huge cauldron on the fire! Where could one get such mouth-watering taste in the U.S.? Certainly not in the burgers and french-fries in McDonalds or Wimpy's!

I saw the Amareswar temple from a distance, its white dome proudly displaying the red and yellow flag of the God Shiva. Ah, the temple and its numerous festivals! The elaborate rituals, the loud music, the frenzied dance by devotees! And the sweetmeats in different shapes! What great excitement! Hey, here was the spot where I had once dropped a packet of sweets and had got a scolding from my dad at home.

And right there at the corner, one December evening I had to stand, holding the hand of the neighbour's daughter, when her mother went inside to worship and got trapped in the crowd for half an hour. Considering that I was nine and she was around seven, the situation had some romantic possibilities, except that she was incredibly clever and calculating. She made me spend each and every penny I had in my pocket, on tid-bits for her. Just as I was getting ready to tell her what beautiful eyes she had, the mother came back and took her away!

I smiled at that sweet memory and started walking again, when suddenly a motorbike cut across the street and stopped before me. A middle-aged, bald, portly man got down, shouting smilingly at me,

"Hey Anupam, how are you?"

I was surprised. Who was this man? Was he a classmate? If so, it must be from the high-school in Cuttack, because my college education was at the Engineering College at Rourkela, three hundred miles away. What was the name of this gentleman? I kept racking my brain, but couldn't place him.

He continued,

"Anupam, don't you remember me? Of course, you must have become a big shot now. Why will you have time for small fries like me?"

I felt embarrassed. I could have asked my friend his name, but he was so effusive and sounded so informal, I didn't have the heart to tell him that I had forgotten his name. With as much confidence as I could muster, I smiled at him.

"Of course, I remember you! Where are you these days?"

I thought it was safer to ask him some neutral questions, to hide my embarrassment of forgetting his name.

"Where else can I go? 'Born in Cuttack, die in Cuttack', that is my motto. You are the brilliant one, to have flown away to America! Our Sanskrit teacher in the school used to call you the jewel of the class! Remember Bikash, the joker of the class? Whenever we meet, he laughs and tells everyone, look at Anupam, went to America, now he must be the jewel in the crown of America! Once a jewel, always a jewel!"

I tried to unfold the thick pages of memory to locate Bikash. A few faces flashed before me. But I was not sure if Bikash was one of them. I tried to continue the thread of our conversation.

"You are the lucky one. Whoever lives in Cuttack is lucky. It is the best place in the world"

"Where in America do you live, Anupam? In Cheecago?'

Only if I could remember his name, I could have told my friend that the city is pronounced as 'Sicago' and not 'Cheecago'! I was still terribly troubled by my inability to recall his name.

"No no, I live in a small place called College Station."

"College? You are still in college, after all these years? Are you still a student? Not doing a job yet?"

"I teach at the University of Texas."

"Anupam! You are a teacher? You mean a master? What a fall for you! You were the topper of the class. All of us thought you will become an I.A.S, phai-A.S. But finally you have landed up as a mere master! And that too in America! What a fall! Arey, compared to you I have done much better! After B.A. I joined my uncle's business as a petty contractor. Today I am an A class contractor, with a fat bank balance!"

I wanted to correct my friend, to tell him that I am not a mere master, but an internationally renowned Professor of Industrial Engineering, I teach university students, guide the research of Ph.D. scholars and I have more than eighty research papers published in reputed journals. But he was so happy about being better off than me, that I didn't have the heart to burst his bubble of joy.

"If you are living in a College are you in a hostel? Don't you have a house of your own?"

"I have a second hand three bedroom house."

"Second hand! Why second hand? And that too only three bedrooms? Look at me. I have eight bedrooms in my house, ground floor and first floor put together!"

"My house is ok. It has a beautiful lawn. My wife and I mow the lawn every week and keep it trim."

The friend screamed at me,

"Mow the lawns! You mean you cut grass? Anupam, you have gone all the way to America to cut grass? What does your wife do? Is she doing a regular job or only cutting grass at home?"

I was taken aback by my friend's unexpected aggressiveness.

"She works at the University as a Technical Assistant in a Laboratory" I bleated.

"But that looks like a small job! Look at my wife. She had joined as an accountant in a bank and now she is an officer drawing a six-figure salary. I have bought a car for her, a Maruti Esteem. After leaving the three children at school the driver drops her at the bank and picks all of them up in the evening."

"You are really lucky to have a driver. In the U.S. we can't afford a driver. So we drive our own cars, drop the kids at school, go to work and do groceries."

"Groceries? You mean you don't have a servant to buy vegetables and groceries for you?"

I almost fainted. Servants? In U.S.? What a crazy thought!

"No, in U.S. no one can afford a servant. We do everything on our own."

"Anupam, Anupam, the topper of the class! What a fall for you! I have two servants at home, one for doing outdoor work and one exclusively to take care of my personal needs. If the fellow doesn't give a massage to me in the night I can't get sleep. And I have a full-time cook and a part-time gardener."

My friend took a breather, wallowing in the self-satisfaction of his successful life.

He continued the attack, trying to rub it in.

"So, you must be sweeping the rooms and cleaning the utensils?"

Before I could reply, he added,

"And you wash your clothes also?"

I felt like telling him that we have a dish-washer, a vacuum-cleaner and a washing machine at home, but somehow I was a bit disoriented with his non-stop questioning. I just nodded my head.

"Who does the daily cooking, you or your wife?"

"We help each other in cooking, but there is no time to cook daily. We cook during the weekends, prepare packets of food and put them in the freezer. Every day we take out a few packets, heat the food and eat."

My friend let out a piercing scream.

"What? What are you saying? Can any decent human being eat food like that? What kind of life are you leading Anupam? What a great fall for you – the topper of the class!

No wonder you are looking so thin and emaciated. Like a starved goat! Look at me; I must have added fifty kilos to my weight in the past ten years. See my healthy body, my smooth face and my round tummy. Anupam, please come to my house tomorrow evening. I will invite Bikash, Biju, Sushil, Ajay and Lokaa – all of them were in school with us. They will be happy to see you. We will have imported whisky and continental food from Akbari Hotel. I will show you what good food means."

I was still desperately trying to remember his name and feeling disturbed about it. Cutting short his enthusiasm, I told him,

"Sorry, I can't come tomorrow evening. I have to leave for Delhi to catch the night flight to U.S. I have been away from my family for ten days, they are waiting for me to return. But I promise, next time when we come, we will visit you and enjoy your hospitality."

"Your family is not here with you? Why have you come alone?"

"It is too expensive for all four of us to come together. Anyway we are now planning a trip for the year after next. We will come....."

Before I could finish, my friend burst out,

"What! You don't have enough money to buy flight tickets for the family! Anupam! What a great fall! What a miserable fall! I can't believe this! Topper of the class! And you don't have money to build a new house, to eat properly, to engage a servant, and even to pay for tickets to visit India! Anupam, it's all a cruel game of fate. Otherwise how could you land in such a mess! Anyway, everyone to his fate! Let me leave,

I am getting late for my construction site. Next time when you come don't forget to give me a call."

The friend shook hands with me and left. I could see a new spring in his gait, a buoyant spirit in his manners. The fact that he was a hugely successful contractor in Cuttack leading a life of luxury whereas the topper of his class was leading a miserable life in far-off U.S. as a mere master, gave him a tremendous boost. I looked at him wistfully. If only I could remember his name, this unexpected meeting would not have been so disappointing for me.

The friend went near his bike, looked at his face in the mirror, combed his hair and turned his leg to sit on the motorcycle. Seeing the way he turned his right leg, I got a jolt. Somehow it looked familiar. And then it came as a bang! His name! My God, this was Shorty! Yes, yes, this was Shorty, no doubt about it. He was almost my height now, and was so portly, but during our school days he was the shortest and skinniest boy in our class. Because of his short height he had a peculiar way of turning his leg to get onto the bicycle. Even today, the style had remained with him! Troubled by the discomfort of the past half an hour, I suddenly felt as if I have won a lottery. In ecstatic joy, I shouted, "Shorty!"

Shorty had started the motorbike. He looked back, flashed a cute smile – it was the same smile of the school days – and waving at me, he rolled away.

I couldn't control my excitement. So this was Shorty! He had changed so much! In our school days he was exceptionally short, almost a foot shorter than others in our class and very thin. He desperately wished to join our gang of the 'adults', but we used to shoo him away with taunts like 'get lost, you mouse' or 'keep drinking Complan and apply next year'! In those heady days of our adolescence, endless hours were spent on talking about the girls in the school, and weaving colourful dreams around them. Often our mind was carried away by the wings of fantasy, reaching the sweet peaks of limitless bliss and melancholic desire. Hearts ached for love and pined for togetherness. Needless to say, those peaks of sweet ecstasy were terribly crowded and immature juveniles like Shorty had no place there.

But we often wondered if Shorty would ever grow up, and lead a normal life! Would Shorty get married? And if he got married would this emaciated weakling be able to fulfill the conjugal obligations that the marital life demands? On a fading afternoon with the sun hiding behind a maze of clouds, a member of our gang raised a crucial issue.

"Abey, how do you know Shorty will not bring dishonour to our class? If he gets married and fails in his conjugal duties, there will be mud on the face of the entire class!"

Someone spotted Shorty at a distance and shouted,

"Abey Shorty, will you get mud on our face?"

Shorty didn't understand and ran away, afraid to face the collective taunt of the gang. Later one of the gang members took him aside and explained the cause of our concern. After that, every time we shouted at him, "Shorty, will you get mud on our face?" Shorty used to flash a broad smile and shake his head to assure us that he was perfectly capable of carrying out his conjugal obligations!

Thinking of Shorty's assertions of those days, I was suddenly seized with a panic. Had Shorty let us down? Had he got mud on our face? Then I remembered him talking about his Maruti Esteem and the driver dropping his three kids at school. I was happy that Shorty had not brought dishonor to our class.

Buoyed by that reassurance, I resumed my walk. Many of the landmarks of my childhood had disappeared, the bakery shop with its effusive aroma of cakes and pastries, the bangle shop displaying an astounding range of colours, the shop with huge calendars and photo-binding facilities, were all gone. But the Prabhat Talkies appeared at a distance. This was where my dad used to take the whole family once in three months to watch movies. I felt as if it was only yesterday that we had all trooped in there to enjoy the patriotic film Jis Desh Mein Ganga Behti Hai.

With Shorty's name, floodgates of the past opened up. The thick layer of dust was swept away from memory, and like rays of sunshine lighting up a dark room with the opening of a window, a thousand pictures flashed before my eyes in rapid succession. The faces of Bikash, Bijay, Sushil and many others appeared like pieces of glittering diamond. So did the lovely and enchanting faces of Dipti, Aparna, Sulekha, Latika and other girls who used to fill our days with the happy colours of Holi and the evenings with the dazzle of Diwali. Suddenly my mind was flooded with memories of the past, its many fantasies and pangs of desire.

I was seized with an intense bout of nostalgia. In my life's eventful journey, each year was like a storey of a building. From the top storeys the past looked like a golden dream, built on the infinite sweetness of a life gone by, leaving a whiff of soft memories. In a swift transformation, I ceased to be the Professor of Industrial Engineering at the University of Texas and became a sixteen-year-old adolescent walking to the school with dreams in my eyes and joy in my heart.

I knew, with the radiance of blessed memories, I would now enter the premises of my school. The air would fill up with the soft giggles of the vibrant girls of my school days, with their glowing cheeks and twinkling eyes. Like a man walking in sleep, I would reach the staircase near the eighth grade classroom and scratch the wall with trembling fingers, to reveal the three magic words of 'I Love You', written by a love-lorn Pramod for the doe-eyed Binodini. Quietly prodded by an invisible force, I would slowly drift towards the playground. From the far corner, out of an old crack in the wall covered with mildew, a torn piece of paper would come floating. I would open it with shaking hands – the cute letter written by the shy Sushil for the ever-giggling Renuka, would smile at me innocently. Mesmerized, I would walk back and enter the tenth grade class room. With soft, gentle footsteps, I, Anupam, the sixteen-year-old dream-struck adolescent, would quietly go and sit at a corner of the first row. Nandini didi, my petite, ever-smiling English teacher would be reciting the lyrics of 'The Solitary Reaper' in her lilting voice. I would sit there, eyes unblinking, lost in a haze of sweet solitude. In that sublime moment of my life, memory would stand still, the sub-conscious mind frozen as a tiny speck in the universe of time.

GLOSSARY

Abey – A form of derogatory address usually among friends

Arey – A form of address denoting close friendship

Baliyatra – An annual fair to celebrate the ancient maritime glory of Orissa

Baraa, aloochap, pakudi, goolgula, baigini, and piaji – Variety of mouth-watering snacks made out of assorted vegetables dipped in a batter of powdered gram flour and fried in oil

Buxi Bazar – One of the old localities of Cuttack town in Orissa

Diwali – The autumn festival of lights when lamps are lit in every home to celebrate the triumph of good over evil

Cuttack – The biggest town of Orissa in Eastern India, with a population of around one million

Gadgadiya Ghat – One of the many bathing points in river Mahanadi in Cuttack

Gulmohar – The Flame of the Forest tree.

Holi – The festival of color in India, celebrated on the arrival of spring

Lassi – Sweetened buttermilk made out of yoghurt, sugar and assorted flavors

Lord Shiva – Shiva is a major Hindu deity, and is the Destroyer or Transformer among the Trimurti, the Hindu Trinity of the primary aspects of the divine

Machhua Bazar – A settlement of fishermen

Manisahu Chhak – A locality named after a prominent businessman of Cuttack

– 5 –

IGLOO

Abhijit sat up. Oh my God! Didn't someone say, to be forewarned is to be forearmed? Nervous, he took a sip from the cup of tea and read again the message from the Daily Horoscope column of The Odisha Times, "Tread cautiously today. Danger is lurking in unexpected corners. Avoid any kind of confrontation. Watch your words. Try to be prudent in dealing with friends and relatives."

A year back Abhijit rarely read the horoscope column in the newspaper, but things had changed suddenly one fine morning. A casual glance at the prediction for Taurus out of idle curiosity and unknowingly he had hit the bull's eye. "A day of unexpected pleasures. Food and drinks fit for a king will be spread on a platter for you. Eat and enjoy, a day like this comes but rarely in life!"

Abhijit had felt like laughing at the bloke writing this ubiquitous column. Food and drinks fit for a king! On a working day! Had this unfortunate bloke tasted the fare Jayanti, his wife dished out! Day after day, night after night! Shortly after their wedding two years back, she had once brought some hot beverage to the breakfast table; Abhijt took a sip and said,

"Darling, it looks so good, but its taste is pleasantly ambiguous. If it is tea, can you please get me some coffee, and if it is coffee, can you get me some tea?"

Being newlywed, he was forgiven, but the laughter of his wife was ominous, carrying a silent but firm message; only once, such a wisecrack, not again! He understood and had been gulping down whatever was offered in the name of food. But unexpected pleasures? Had it been a Sunday or a holiday he would have taken Jayanti out to some restaurant for a dinner fit for a king, but not on a working day when he would return from his bank around nine. As the manager of a branch, he had to reconcile all the entries, account for the cash, lock up the strong room and leave around eight thirty to reach home at nine.

But, Mr. Astrologer was right. At lunch time he got a call from Pradip, his class mate from college who was visiting from the U.S.; he invited Abhijit to dinner with spouse, along with Arabind and Gokul, two other friends. They met at Hotel Mayfair at eight and over four bottles of Californian wine brought by Pradip, they had mutton biriyani, chicken tangdi kebab, fish cutlet and prawn masala, followed by the best rasmalai and pudding a chef could produce! A feast fit for a king! Hah, Mr. Astrologer, you are too conservative, it was a meal fit for an emperor, a king of kings!

After that Abhijit got addicted to the horoscope column. Six months later the prediction in the horoscope again hit the bull's eye!

"Money from unexpected quarters, possibly through acquisition of immovable property. Overseas communication is likely, keep your options open."

Options? Why options, Abhijit thought: for acquisition of money, he could keep his whole heart open, like a dissected watermelon.

At two in the afternoon someone called from the village; an elderly relative had kicked the bucket an hour back. His only son was in the U.S., who had no time for the poor father in India, busy as he was in earning his dollars in the country of the greenbacks. The elderly relative, Biranchi Chacha had to undergo repeated surgeries for an abdominal cancer last year. He had come to Bhubaneswar for chemotherapy and stayed with Abhijeet's family. Jayanti took care of him. The old man had to come repeatedly and felt immensely grateful to Abhijeet and Jayanti for their care and devotion.

On getting the news Abhijeet took half a day's leave and rushed to the nearest internet centre to call Biranchi Chacha's son in the U.S. Lalu Bhaina was aghast at being disturbed at four in the morning,

"How dare you disturb me at this ungodly hour? Don't you know when it is two thirty in your India, U.S. time here is four in the morning?"

Abhijeet was shocked at this outburst. When he broke the news, Bhaina refused to come immediately,

"How can I go? It's not like your India, just push off, leaving an application! You want me to lose my job? And your Bhabhi just can't go; children are in the thick of their semester. Listen, you and your wife can do all the rituals. You are our caste, right? I will come for three four days towards the end. Don't worry, take leave from your job, I will compensate you for all that you do. Okay? Now let me go back to my sleep. I have two important client's meetings today. And one thing, Abhi, in future if you call me, remember there is a ten and half-hours' time difference between your country and the U.S."

Lalu Bhaina banged the phone down. Abhijeet felt drained. What a way to mourn one's father's death! On the way home he suddenly recalled the conversation and realised Lalu Bhaina hadn't even had the time to ask what the problem with his father was and how he had died!

Since Biranchi Chacha had no other child Abhijeet and Jayanti carried out the funeral and performed all the rituals. Lalu Bhaina came on the eighth day and participated in the ceremonies. Abhijeet was seeing him after twenty three years. He had almost forgotten his Odiya accent and spoke mostly in American English; even his Odiya sounded like that, liberally sprinkled with, 'you know', 'tell you what', 'say that again', 'awesome', 'Jeesuss', 'Lord bless my soul' and all that. On the second day, he sat down with Abhijeet and asked him what would be the best way to sell off the house and land in the village and what price it would fetch.

"Now that I am an American citizen, there is no point in holding on to this property in India, you know. It will be like unwanted butter on a burnt out bread, you see."

Abhijeet said he would check on the sale price of land and let Lalu Bhaina know.

"Yes, yes, do that. You can charge a little commission for that also. In U.S. we don't believe in getting free services from any one. There is a price for everything, you know. Like, you work, you get paid. No hanky panky like your miserable India."

That evening Lalu Bhaina invited Abhijeet to help him in arranging the things in the house, sort out all the papers "and throw away all that awful garbage, you know." And then the bomb exploded! In the second drawer of the old table, they found a Will executed by Biranchi Chacha bequeathing all his property to Abhijeet and Jayanti. There was a letter also for Lalu Bhaina, lamenting the fact that the son was so busy earning his dollars that he never had time to call his father, and that the grand kids, well into their teens, had never visited India to meet their grandfather. The selfless care and love given by Abhijeet and Jayanti made him feel as if they were his real children; hence the property was bequeathed to them. Lalu Bhaina flew into a rage, his face got red and eyes became evil. It appeared as if he would pounce upon Abhijeet and tear him to pieces. "So? It's now clear you and Jayanti are dangerous snakes, biting the hand that feeds you! All this drama of selfless service was to get the property, wasn't it? How cleverly you tricked him to give away his property worth lakhs to you? And the old fool, he didn't think of the love we have for him. And his grandchildren, why should they carry the old man's surname? Once I go home I will change those surnames. Now, get out of my sight. I don't want to talk to you again."

Lalu Bhaina didn't talk to Abhijeet again for the next two days and quietly slipped away after the tenth day ceremony was over. Abhijeet realised the prediction in the horoscope column of the newspaper was true, though it involved unpleasant situations.

Three months after that, Abhijeet's mind filled with a mild excitement when he read the horoscope column. "A pleasant day. Romance in the air! Keep flowers and music ready. Loosen the purse strings if you want to get the best out of it." Abhijeet smiled to himself. Ah, romance! Should he take a day off? He and Jayanti could have lunch in a restaurant and then go to a movie! Then he remembered the Audit team was visiting the branch and his presence was essential. Anyway he would try to return early and they could go for dinner late in the evening. And if not anything else, night could be made romantic with a few flowers on the bed and a range of passion could shine like the colours of a rainbow!

Throughout the day Abhijeet's mind remained mildly intoxicated. On the way home he bought some flowers. He wanted the prediction of romance to come true. To his surprise Jayanti opened the door with a red saree covering her head and half her face. Ah, the fever of romance! So contagious! He presented the flowers to her and lifted the veil from the face wanting to gather her in a tight hug. The next moment, he recoiled, as if bit by a snake! Who was this lady, opening the door to him and now giggling like a school girl! She broke into an uncontrollable laugh, like a woman possessed, and from the loud laughter Abhijeet recognised her. Sulata! Jayanti's cousin, the ever playful, naughty, flirty, seductive beauty! When had she come? She must have come during the day and the two sisters must have kept it a secret, to spring a surprise on the unsuspecting Abhijeet!

Abhijeet smiled and gave a small pat on Sulata's cheek.

"You scared me; I thought I had entered the wrong house!"

"Ah, Jiju, look at my fate, I was waiting for a hug from you, but missed it by a whisker. It has been always like that. Remember your wedding day?"

Abhijeet started laughing. Of course he remembered! On the wedding day he was smothered by a dozen sisters-in-law of all ages, sizes and colours, Sulata was the loudest and naughtiest among them. The wedding was over and the bride sat in another room holding small kowries in her hand, waiting for the husband to open her hands and take away the kowries. When Abhijeet held her hand, his first touch of the freshly minted wife, the bride started laughing and rolled unto the ground. From under the saree a pair of jeans peeped out, the veil slid off. It was Sulata, laughing like a horse and shouting, "Hai, hai, my bad luck, if I had not laughed and rolled unto the ground Jiju would not have known and tonight in the bridal chamber he would have lifted my veil and sung, Suhaag Raat hey, ghunghat utha rahahoon mein." She started singing the song loudly, in her thick manly voice and all the other girls started punching her and tickling her till she ran away.

Next year it was her turn to get married and there was so much fun! She married a doctor and they were living three hundred miles away in a small town. Sulata was still the best friend of Jayanti and the two sisters used to spend hours over telephone talking and exchanging all kinds of gossip. Today her husband had dropped her at Jayanti's place and gone off to Delhi to attend some conference for two days. They had dinner at home, Sulata talking all the time and pulling Abhijeet's leg, playing pranks like she was still the Sulata who wanted him to lift her ghunghat in the bridal chamber. Jayanti enjoyed the discomfiture of Abhijeet and the three of them talked till late into the night. The next day Abhijeet was in a great mood, buoyed by non-stop praise and adulation by Sulata; his handsome personality, his shy nature, and his gentlemanly manners all coming for high appreciation from her. Jayanti also joined in the banter and by the time he left for the bank, he felt like a bird flying in the sky trying to touch its blueness and its vast splendour. In the evening they went to watch a movie, Sulata cracking jokes all the time.

"Jiju, be careful, don't try anything naughty with Didi in the dark. You are under watch."

Abhijeet asked her, "Why, what does Subhash do in movie halls with you?"

"Oh, he is a thorough professional, like a good doctor he examines my body once the lights go off."

And she broke into loud giggles, winking at Abhijeet in a lurid way. The movie got over quite late, they had dinner at home. The next evening they went to Pushpak hotel for dinner. Abhijeet ordered good, mouth-watering dishes for his 'charming Saali' and she ordered exotic ice cream for her 'darling Jiju'. She kept on praising him for the excellent choice of dishes, for being so smart and handsome and for being 'God's gift to Jayanti didi'. She licked the bar of Heavenly Delight and handed it over to Jiju, who licked it like it was Manna from heaven. He handed over his cup of Cream of Passion to Sulata, who rolled her eyes and said 'Fantabulous'! Jayanti watched this fun and frolic with a fixed smile on her face. Neither the Jiju, nor the Sali offered her a bite of their ice cream. On the way home Jayanti was unusually silent, but Sulata and Abhijeet kept exchanging banter and laughing all the time. The chemistry between the handsome Jiju and the rollicking Saali was getting stronger by the minute.

Subhash was to return at eleven in the morning and they were to drive off to Baripada after lunch. Before going off to sleep Abhijeet suggested the two sisters should go the market in the morning and buy a saree for Sulata. Jayanti snapped at him,

"No need, her husband is a doctor, they have enough money to buy sarees for Sulata."

Abhijeet went off to sleep, dreaming of colourful ice cream bars, wrapped in sizzling noodles and dripping droplets of honey. The next morning before leaving for the bank, he invited Sulata to visit again, reminding her of the nice time they all had, thanks to her sweet nature and cute manners.

That was three months back. Abhijeet's faith on the predictions in the daily horoscope had gone up tremendously after the pleasant romantic interlude with Sulata. Today the warning about impending confrontations unnerved him. He sought Jayanti's help in overcoming the dangers associated with his mercurial nature, his tendency to get angry at the slightest pretext. She smiled and said she understood. She promised to call him a couple of times during the day and remind him of the warning. At breakfast Abhijeet crossed the first huddle. The upma was extra salty, Abhijeet wanted to ask if makers of Tata Salt were having a scheme of Buy one Get one free. But at the last second he remembered the warning and held himself back. Today was not a day to play with Jayanti's sentiments.

At the bank there was a minor pandemonium when he reached; the cashier had not turned up and a crowd was forming at the counter. He called the cashier's home and was told that he had been taken ill. He wanted to shout at the bloke that he should have called and informed the bank. But Abhijeet restrained himself; the cashier was the General Secretary of the Bank Employees' Union and today was not the day to rake up a fight with him, not after what the horoscope said.

At eleven thirty Mrs. Samal stormed into his room. The old professor had been a pain in the neck for the past two years, ever since Abhijeet had joined as the Manager. Today she was picking up a fight on why she should fill a form for the Live Certificate to continue her pension. She just looked at Abhijeet and said, 'I am, so I exist'. Abhijeet had been suffering from her tantrums for a long time and he wanted to hold her by her fat neck and squeeze the life out of her, but remembering the warning in the horoscope column, he hid his potentially maniac hand under the table, sported a plastic smile and asked the Assistant Manager to fill up the form on her behalf.

An hour later the local MLA stormed in with a few hangers-on and started firing straight away,

"How dare you issue a notice to Jitendra Swain? Don't you know he is my right hand man? Is he the only defaulter in your branch? Is it your father's money you are giving as loan? It is our money, the people's money. How dare you? How dare you….."

On any other day Abhijeet would have started an argument with the MLA, who was talking as if the Manager of a bank was his father's servant. But no, not today, of all the days. The warning was lurking in his mind. He simply promised to look into the matter; it was not possible to do it today because the computer was down. The MLA left with a parting shot,

"Yes, you better do it, unless you want to be transferred to some remote branch in a Naxal-affected area. Remember, we are the masters of the people, you are only paid servants!"

Abhijeet badly wanted to speak to someone; he called Jayanti and spoke to her. She asked him to keep patience and somehow see the day through, may be tomorrow would be a better day. In the evening Abhijeet went to preside over a loan mela, where his branch was disbursing loans to the weaker sections of the society. The Chief Guest was the President of a local NGO, who had a few scores to settle with Abhijeet. The function went on for two hours; many from the local area were grateful to the bank for giving them the financial assistance.

The President of the NGO was not convinced. He looked pointedly at Abhijeet while giving his speech and fired shot after shot at self-centered, arrogant Bank Managers who sit in air-conditioned rooms and don't feel the pulse of the people. Abhijeet wanted to tell the audience how 'unselfish' the President was and the kind of beneficiaries he had sponsored. But somehow he didn't want to pick up a fight. He had been treading cautiously, as advised by Mr. Astrologer and didn't want to take a risk late in the evening.

He came home, all smiles, and gave a big hug to Jayanti. Over dinner they went through the events of the day and were happy that Abhijeet had come out of the day's ordeals unscathed. Jayanti smiled and reminded him how many times she had prayed during the day for Abhijeet. She was getting increasingly lovey-dovey, the night promised to be romantic. Time to plan a child, Abhijeet told himself. They went to bed, Jayanti remembered the quarrelsome Professor, smiled and just to tease Abhijeet, she said, "I am, so I exist". She tickled him and brought him to a romantic crescendo. Abhijeet realised that she was getting more and more flirtatious. Flirtatious! He suddenly remembered Sulata, who had called during the day. He thought he would break the news to Jayanti,

"Oh, I forgot to tell you. Sulata had called, she said she tried your number but it was continuously busy. Her husband Subhash is again going to Delhi for two days and she is coming to stay with us next week. She was very excited, she made me promise I will take leave for a day and the three of us will go to visit Nandan Kanan, the beautiful zoo on the outskirts of Bhubaneswar."

Jayanti had suddenly become silent, all playfulness gone in a minute.

"Why does she want to go to Nandan Kanan? I can't go with her. She has become insufferable, blabbering all the time. Last time she talked so much, I got a headache!"

Abhijeet was still riding the crest of a rising romance, "O, O, I thought she is your most favourite sister! OK, if you don't want to go, I will take my cute Saali for an outing at Nandan Kanan."

Suddenly the room became still, gripped by a palpable tension. Jayanti froze, moved away from Abhijeet and went off to sleep facing the wall. Abhijeet heaved a deep sigh, he felt as if the room had become cold, very cold, an Igloo, and Jaynti's breath was hanging like heartless icicles suspended from a stone-cold roof.

GLOSSARY

Chacha – Uncle

Ghunghat – Veil

Jiju – Sister's husband

Kowrie – Small conch-like shells used during wedding rituals

Saali – Wife's sister

Suhaag Raat Hei .... – A popular Hindi song to describe the honeymoon of newlywed

– 6 –

THE FLAME

Snehlata adjusted the tie on her husband's shirt and gave him a small pat on the cheek,

"Oye, what has happened to you these days? You are super careful while leaving for office, the perfume, the gel on the hair, the trimmed moustache? Some new flame in the office?"

Ramesh Patnaik's heart skipped a beat! Wives! Blast their sixth sense! The next moment he steadied himself and patted her back,

"You only have taught me to be smart and sprightly all the time. After all Odisha Government's Tourism Secretary has to present himself to the world with a flourish and glamour! Now let me leave. It's getting late. God knows who would be waiting for me! Tourism department is going places now! And look at you, all you can think of is a flame!"

✳ ✳ ✳

The "Flame", at that precise moment, was walking briskly from the bus stand to the Secretariat. She was nervous, just a month into the job she didn't want to incur the displeasure of the boss. Anima was the Junior P.A. to the Tourism Secretary. She knew the moment Sir came to office, he would send for her and if she had not reached, he would shout at the Senior P.A. Banamali Garabadu. Wasn't he teaching office discipline to his junior? Why was she coming late to office? Banamali babu, the seasoned P.A. would sense the impatience of the colourful boss to see the blooming flower which had fallen into the office like a gift from Cupid. He would be aware that it was not yet ten o clock, Anima was not late, only in his eagerness to see her on a Monday morning, Sir had come to office ten minutes early. But being an expert in handling bosses he would say,

"She must be on the way, Sir, a very efficient and capable lady, perfect in typing and dictation".

Ramesh Patnaik would snort in impatience,

"Yes, yes, I know that, I know that. Send her in, the moment she comes, for dictation".

"If there is anything urgent, I can take the dictation Sir."

"No, no, you attend to phone calls, let her take dictation."

✻✻✻

Dictation? Of course the boss knew Banamali babu was very seasoned and good in dictation. In fact he was good in everything. Actually, Ramesh Patnaik liked him a lot. A humble, God fearing old man, he would bend from the waist in the morning and evening while saying Namaskar to the boss. He would give the impression that the boss was God, as much to be revered as the gods and goddesses adorning the framed photo in the wall in the entrance room. Banamali Garabadu was efficiency personified. Anything that the boss wanted was done in a jiffy. Madam wanted to go shopping for sarees, Banamali Babu would call the show room and alert them; fifteen year old son Mayank wanted to go on a picnic with his friends to Konark, the efficient PA would make all arrangements; twelve year old daughter Sharanya forgot to remind about payment of school fees, no problem, Banamali Babu would rush to the school and pay the fees without late fee. But still, Ramesh Patnaik hungered for the young, nubile Anima, not for the old, efficient Banamali Babu.

✳ ✳ ✳

Banamali Babu knew there was nothing urgent. The same boss never used to bother with dictation when Sanatan was the Junior P.A. Ever since Anima had joined in the place of Sanatan, Sir is overflowing with new ideas and unending dictation. This eager man in his mid-forties was quite a handful, his eyes wandering over Anima's sensuous body left no one in doubt about what must be going on in his dirty mind.

✳ ✳ ✳

The mind of Ramesh Patnaik was in a turmoil, why was Anima late? Had something happened to her? Impatient, he looked at the clock. It was five minutes past ten and Anima had still not come in. He had been thinking of her all the way to office. What colour saree would she be wearing today? The yellow chiffon with the green dots which hugs her slim figure so nicely, accentuating the gentle curves, or the light green cotton saree which sits on her like a soft veil or the violet one which suits her fair colour so well? Would she have left her hair undone or tied it into a bun? And the bindi on her forehead, would it be a round one or of a small diamond shape? Whatever she wore she looked ravishing, a succulent fruit waiting to be enjoyed with relish.

He was waiting to spend a good one hour with her pretending to give dictation, thinking of words and officialese but actually looking at her sitting demurely, eyes downcast and lips trembling like the tremor of soft rose petals. The moment she came in Ramesh Patnaik would say,

"Come, come Anima, I have been waiting for you, sit and take a dictation about my programme for today".

"11 am - Telephone call to JS, Ministry of Tourism, Govt. of India

No no, make it AS, let me speak to the Additional Secretary, or you think JS will be better? Ok, keep it JS.

11.30 - Speak to batch mate Anil Mahajan about Trade Fair in Patna.

But is it a bit early, Trade Fair is still six months away. Last year Trade Fair was in Bangalore, remind me to check the file to find out when we started the process.

12.30 pm - Dictation

1.30 - Lunch in office

3.00 - Meeting with AS and US in charge of Light and Sound show at Dhauligiri.

Or should I finish the beautification of Sisupalagarh first? When you go from here ask Banamali babu to connect me to MD Tourism. Let me check the progress with him.

4.30 Dictation"

Ramesh Patnaik would be fantasising in his mind all the while. Ah, Anima, leave all this useless stuff. Let's change the whole programme to 11 am - Clearing Files assisted by

Ms. Anima, Junior P.A. 12.30 Dictation to Anima. 1.30 Lunch with Anima (Special lunch of Biriyani and Fish Fry to be ordered by the office from Pantha Nivas, the government owned tourism hotel.) 3.30 Dictation to Anima. 5 pm Tea with Anima. *(I know you don't like tea, but all that you have to do is, touch the cup with your sweet lips and hand it over to me, I will sip it drop by drop like it was nectar from heaven. Ah, when will you give me that chance Anima, when?)*

* * *

When will Sir let me go, Anima was getting restless. For the past forty five minutes he had been dictating his programme for the day, saying something, changing it, repeating it, asking her for her opinion as if she was a fountainhead of knowledge. Anima had no doubt about the dirty intention of her boss. Being exceptionally beautiful she was always an object of unwelcome attention from class mates and unscrupulous professors, but she had managed to ward off all kinds of danger by being aloof, travelling by ladies' special buses and avoiding offers of lift from class mates in their scooters or motorbikes. She knew she would be subject to such harassment till she got married. Actually she herself wanted to get married, but she had to save some money from her salary for the marriage. She knew her father who was a retired school teacher had already spent all his savings on the marriage of her two elder sisters.

Ramesh Patnaik looked at her with naked hunger gleaming in his eyes. In a sky-coloured saree with deep red borders she was looking just out of the world. Should he ask her to join him for lunch? Ah, what a joy that would be! Next moment he was assailed by a doubt, would she agree?

These days with all the Me Too scandals, what if she told everyone that he was trying to force a piece of fish fry into her dainty mouth? Anyway, let him order the fish fry first.

Anima came out of her reverie when the boss pressed the intercom and ordered fish fry from Pantha Nivas. Two plates of fish fry.

***

Fish fry? Banamali babu was surprised. He knew Sir had a problem of irritable bowel syndrome and that's why madam sent only plain rice and non- spicy dishes from home. Why did he order fish fry from Pantha Nivas? And two plates? Is he expecting guests at lunch? When Anima came in after dictation he asked her was Sir talking to someone on the mobile, had he invited someone for lunch? She shook her head; she hadn't heard anything of the sort. But she certainly heard him asking Banamali babu to get fish fry from Pantha Nivas.

***

Pantha Nivas? Anima had heard about the hotel from others. How big would be the rooms? She imagined the rooms, coloured walls, white bed sheets, good sofa sets. When she got married she would probably have the wedding in Pantha Nivas. As the Junior PA to the Tourism Secretary she would try to get special service. In all innocence she asked Banamali Babu,

"Sir, how big is Pantha Nivas? How many rooms are there? How is the food? Is it a good place to have a marriage?"

Banamali Babu looked at her in amusement,

"Are you getting married? You haven't told us so far? Where is the mithai? Who is the lucky man? To get an apsara like you as a wife?"

Anima blushed a deep red, as deep as the border of her saree,

"No, no, it's for a class mate of mine. She was enquiring the other day"

Banamali babu teased her,

"Why only the class mate, even for you also we will make all arrangements in Pantha Nivas. The manager calls me for something or the other three times every day. Last year I had got my daughter's wedding conducted there. They gave me a hefty discount and took special care to make all arrangements, from wedding to reception to honeymoon".

The old man's face broke into a wicked smile and he looked pointedly at Anima, who blushed an even deeper red at the word honeymoon.

✳✳✳

Honeymoon? Isn't it too early to think of honeymoon? Let her first decide about her marriage, which is probably still two years away. But no harm in taking a look at Pantha Nivas. Anima smiled to herself, may be as the Tourism Secretary's P.A. she would ask for the biggest suite there for her honeymoon. She blushed again and was aware of the intense gaze of Banamali babu at her face. She looked at him and said,

"Sir, can we go and have a look at Pantha Nivas one of these days? I am just curious to know how the best hotel of the government looks and feels".

"Yes, of course. Sir is going to Delhi for three days on Wednesday. His flight is at two in the afternoon. So he won't come to office, or even if he comes he will leave by the noon. We will visit Pantha Nivas that day. I will ask the Manager to be present and take us round. We will have lunch also, courtesy, Odisha Tourism Development Corporation. I will ask them to make Mutton Biriyani and Fish fry. Hope you like them. Don't bring lunch from home on Wednesday."

Anima hadn't known the Boss would be away for three days. Good riddance from dictation of Sir!

***

Sir had pressed the buzzer. Banamali babu lifted the receiver,

"Yes Sir?"

"What happened to the flight ticket? Have the Pantha Nivas people delivered it?"

"Sir, it must be on the way. I had reminded the Manager in the morning. It seems the Area Manager for the Beverage company has changed, so it's taking a little longer. But the manager of Pantha Nivas has promised to send it today without fail Sir. Rest assured Sir"

"Ok, ok, don't forget to take copies of the ticket. Claim it correctly in the TA bill. It should be around forty four thousand rupees."

"Yes Sir, forty four thousand three hundred seventy two sir, I have already noted it for the TA bill."

"Good, let me know as soon as you receive the ticket."

***

The ticket? Anima was looking questioningly at Banamali babu. She asked him,

"Sir? The ticket is coming from Pantha Nivas?"

"Yes. It always comes from there."

"But you told Sir you will claim it in TA bill? If Pantha Nivas is paying for the ticket why are you claiming it in Sir's TA bill?"

Banamali babu laughed loudly,

"Oh my God, what an innocent little babe you are! Wait, you will learn a lot of things in due course. Arey Pagli, you think Pantha Nivas is paying for it? They will always make the beverage contractor, the civil contractor or the catering contractor to buy the ticket. And since this is a government tour Sir claims it in his TA bill. Forty four thousand is just pocket money for him!"

Anima was horrified,

"But Sir, this is wrong! Why should Boss claim the amount if he has not spent it? And you are such a religious person, with a prominent mark of chandan on your forehead, burning incense sticks in the morning before the photograph of Maa Saraswati, Ganesh and Maa Laxmi on the wall. Why are you being a party to this immoral act?"

Banamali babu's laughter got even louder,

"Aha, aha, such innocence! Straight from the university, aren't you? That's why you don't know the ways of the world!"

✳✳✳

Ways of the world? What ways of the world? Do such things really happen? Anima couldn't resist asking,

"What else happens around here, Sir?"

"Oh, a lot. Our boss often throws parties at Pantha Nivas for his friends and colleagues. Not a single paise goes out of his pocket. I was once P. A. to another very senior officer. Every month he would organise parties in big hotels with unlimited flow of drinks and sumptuous food. The PRO of some Industry or Businessman would be waiting in the wings to pick up the bill which would be in lakhs."

Anima couldn't believe this,

"Are all officers like this?"

"O no, not all are like this, but those who host small parties at home are ridiculed by their friends. After all who is interested in lime-soda, boiled peanuts and fried pakodas? Where is the comparison with scotch whiskey, vodka, chicken tikka, sheek kebabs and prawn fries that you get in hotels? Once I was asked to contact a few officers for a party at home by one of my bosses. Out of eight persons I contacted only one agreed to come. The others had no interest in a party at home."

✳✳✳

Home? Anima remembered there was a call from home when she was with Sir taking dictation. She opened the mobile, it was her brother Aniket. He had run into a small problem. In his B.A. Certificate his name had been misspelt as Anicut, it must have been due to some spell-check issue and he had been running to the College to get it corrected, but the clerk there was only smiling at him, without making any attempt to correct it. She called Aniket at home, he again expressed his anger and sadness. She said she would check what could be done.

Banamali Babu had heard her part of the conversation, he asked her,

"Any problem Anima? We are colleagues - your problem is mine and mine is yours. Tell me, anything I can do?"

She told him, he was surprised,

"We have been seeing each other for the past one month, but you never told me; am I such a bad person, not fit to know about your problems? Now leave it to me. My friend Ajay's brother-in- law is the Section Officer in BJB college, we meet often over sumptuous lunches of mutton curry and fish fry. Let me talk to him."

Sir was busy on the phone talking to the JS in Delhi. Banamali babu called on his mobile, Ghanashyam picked up the phone on the first ring,

"Hello Bhaina, pranam, saashtang pranam, long time no meet!"

"Meat? Didn't we have meat curry at my home last week? Now it is your turn, get some crab from Chilika next week. Ajay and I will come to your place. Now, leave the meat shit business, I have some work with you".

"Work, Bhaina, what work, just order me, I will walk on my head and come over to you to deliver."

Banamali babu gave the phone to Anima, she explained the problem to Ghanashyam and handed back the phone to Banamali Babu.

"Bhaina, what has this world come to? If my clerk smiles and smiles and doesn't do it, madam's brother should understand what needs to be done. Anyway tell her the work is done, a free service from Ghanashyam to his big brother. Let Aniket come and collect the corrected certificate tomorrow afternoon. And this Sunday crab lunch at my place, ok Bhaina?"

Banamali babu ended the call and looked at Anima. Her face was glowing with happiness and relief. Such a cute, graceful girl! He looked forward to Wednesday when he would be taking her for lunch to Pantha Nivas. The buzzer sounded again, Sir wanted Anima to come in for dictation.

✳ ✳ ✳

The dictation meandered for one hour, with nothing particular. Some routine letters and useless notes for the subordinates. Ramesh Patnaik was getting absent minded again and again wondering whether he should invite Anima to join him for lunch. Banamali Babu had already informed that the fish fry had been delivered from Pantha Nivas. Sir was looking at Anima, sweat beads had started forming on his face, looking at Anima and being torn in a dilemma. Anima looked at her watch, it was nearing one thirty, sir had been silent for almost two minutes, he was just looking at her and looking away, something was troubling him. She asked him very softly,

"Sir, if the dictation is over, can I leave? Today all the newly joined Junior P.A.s have been called for a debriefing by the G.A. department secretary over lunch. It is at 1.30. Can I go Sir?"

Suddenly Ramesh Patnaik felt relieved, all tension hooshed away like air from a balloon. So he was no longer in a dilemma. Anima was going for lunch elsewhere. May be he would think of giving her a lunch after his return from Delhi.

✳✳✳

Delhi had no particular attraction for Ramesh Patnaik. It was a waste of three days when there was a Delhi tour. He was not keen on attending the Review Meeting. The Ministry of Tourism had granted 30 crores for the beautification of Puri beach seven years back. The contract was awarded to the brother-in-law of the then Tourism Minister who was now the Revenue Minister. He spent just two crores and misappropriated the balance amount. Five review meetings had already taken place with no progress at all. Who would recover the amount from the mighty Minister's powerful brother in law, now an MLA? The only attraction for the Delhi trip for Ramesh Patnaik was the forty four thousand he would pocket as the airfare.

But the flight from Bhubaneswar leaves at 2.10 pm. While returning it arrives at 1.30 pm. At normal times Ramesh Patnaik would have skipped office for all the three days, but the prospect of seeing Anima would bring him to office for a few hours both on Wednesday and Friday. And he would spend the whole time giving her dictation!

✳✳✳

Dictation! Can he take Anima with him to Delhi on the pretext of giving urgent dictation? Ah, Delhi trip would be memorable if he could do that. Why, he may take her to Agra to show her Taj Mahal also, the monument to eternal love! But could he really take her to Delhi? With the press fellows hounding news like bloody dogs it could become a big scandal!

And Anima? Would she agree to come? Isn't it a little too early to expect her to accompany him to Delhi? May be he would instead get a good gift for her from Delhi! A necklace? Wow, that would be fabulous and would certainly tilt the scale for him, but Snehlata had this annoying habit of checking his credit card bills! Ok, ok, a good perfume paid by cash would perhaps be safer. May be he would try to touch her hand and feel its softness when he handed over the bottle of perfume to her. He smiled to himself at the prospect!

✳✳✳

The prospect of three days of freedom from Sir's dictation had made Anima light-headed the next day. If she could just breeze through this Tuesday, she would enjoy the next three days. She was looking forward to the visit to Pantha Nivas on Wednesday. Banamali Babu was the first one to see a spring in her step when she entered the office.

"Anima, you look so happy! Any particular reason?" He asked her.

"Sir is going away for three days, this is the first time I will be free from work. No buzzer, no dictation!"

Banamali Babu laughed loudly. Sir had not yet come to office; before Anima was called away for dictation he could talk freely to her,

"You are a young, beautiful, sensitive girl, like a fresh flower from the garden. You must have sensed by now why he calls you all the time for dictation?"

Anima looked down and nodded, yes, she knew.

Banamali babu, the old veteran, told her he had worked under another colourful boss like this many years back. He was a poet and romantic feelings were oozing out of him like tooth paste from a leaking tube. Those days Banamali babu was a Junior P.A. and the forty year old Pratima was the Senior P.A. She was a comely, lively spinster and was enamoured by the poems recited by the boss. She fell for him like a slim, shiny fish for a wiggling bait and sank hook, line and sinker. Sir went to Gopalpur on a tour and took her with him. And at the beach guest house they remained engrossed in the poetry of love till the boss's wife reached there from Bhubaneswar and severely beat them up with a chappal. The boss returned to office the next day, but Pratima went on long leave and was transferred out to a far off district headquarters.

After a long time Banamali babu was seeing a lecherous boss again.

Anima shuddered. The thought of accompanying Sir anywhere sickened her, boss or no boss!

✳ ✳ ✳

The boss barged in. Everyone stood up and greeted him and the gentleman accompanying him. His face lighted up like a colourful lamp as his eyes briefly swept over Anima, she was looking like a ripe pomegranate in her red saree and the red dot on the forehead. The unwelcome batchmate of his, the Tribal Affairs Secretary, had met him in the lift and walked in with him. The idiot! Did he know how much precious dictation time he would be taking away? He started listening to the endless chatter of his batch mate, although nothing was registering in his mind, covered with a blanket of cloud.

✳ ✳ ✳

A cloud had come over Anima's face also. The chirpiness was gone when the boss had walked in. Now she was weighed down by a problem she had brought from home. Her father had asked Anima to go over to the DPI's office today to get his pension papers cleared. Although he had retired six months back he was still getting provisional pension only, some query or the other was holding up the final clearance. He was tired of going to the DPI's office again and again. He had heard that one had to pay ten percent of the lump sum benefits to get his pension cleared, but he didn't know whom to offer or how. He thought Anima could go over and try her luck.

She asked Banamali Babu,

"Sir I have to go to the DPI's office for an hour today. Can I go when the Secretary Sir goes for the monthly review meeting with the Chief Secretary?"

"Yes, of course you can go. But why are you going there? It is a den of corruption and young and beautiful girls like you should not go there to get corrupted!"

Anima blushed, this was the second time in half an hour the Senior P.A. was calling her young and beautiful!

"My father's pension papers are stuck there. He had retired as a teacher from a government school six months back, But he is getting only provisional pension. I want to go and check what is holding it up."

Banamali Babu laughed, one of those knowing, condescending laughs he bestows on people ignorant of government business.

"I know what must be holding it up. You don't have to go there, why should you give pains to your dainty feet when I am sitting here, sharing this cabin with you? The PS to the DPI is my batch mate in the stenographer recruitment, we had shared so many samosas and rasagollas together in our youth. Just write down the details on a piece of paper. Let me call him."

After ten minutes he smiled at Anima in Mother Teresa style, all beaming with love and kindness,

"Tell your father to go and meet Abani Puhana, PS to DPI at ten o clock tomorrow. His work will be done in three days. When Abani promises something, it is final."

Anima almost fell off her chair,

"Sir, you have taken away such a load from my mind! Is there anything, anything, that you cannot get done? You are a genius!"

Banamali Babu gloated. In his younger days such words from a dazzling beauty would have flooded him with pleasant waves all over, causing goosebumps! He allowed his mind to tickle itself to a mild fantasy. Tomorrow he would enjoy the company of this innocent beauty for a few hours going around in Pantha Nivas and having a sumptuous lunch followed by fabulous ice cream! For a moment he closed his eyes.

✳ ✳ ✳

His eyes going repeatedly to the wall clock, Ramesh Patnaik finally got rid of his batch mate and immediately sent for Anima. For some reason she looked happy and buoyant. While going through the motion of unnecessary and inane dictations, he wanted to ask her, what made her so bubbly, would she miss him as much as he would miss her when he went away to Delhi. He even thought of asking her what gift she wanted from Delhi, but thought the better of it. He wanted to give her a surprise, a bottle of costly perfume.

***

The perfume bottle neatly packed and tucked into his briefcase, Ramesh Patnaik walked into the office on Friday afternoon, eager, impatient, restless. God knows how much he had missed the sweet, innocent face of the young and nubile Anima in the last three days. He wanted to hand over the bottle of perfume to her, look deep into her eyes and tell her how much he had missed her! He pressed the buzzer,

"Where is Anima? I didn't see her at her desk?"

"Sir, she called in the morning and asked for a day's leave. She is unwell Sir, but she said she would be back on Monday. There are two urgent letters Sir, should I come for taking dictation?"

Ramesh Patnaik slammed the phone down. He felt shattered; shouldn't Anima have called him on his mobile and asked for leave? Should she not confide in him? Now he wouldn't see her till Monday! And he wanted so much to touch her hand today while handing over the perfume bottle! He took out the bottle and carefully hid it in the drawer, locking it firmly. Too explosive to take home! For Snehlata he had bought some mixture and pastries.

He called the peon and asked him to get the car ready. He wanted to go home and take rest.

***

Rest? Snehlata was worried. Why did her husband want to take rest? It was so unlike him! Did something untoward happen in Delhi? He was looking so downcast and haggard! He had not even changed into his customary kurta pyjama before going to bed. She went near him, he was looking vacantly at the roof. Ramesh Patnaik was debating in his mind whether he should call Anima's number and ask her what was the problem, what illness she was suffering from. But what if she was really ill and someone else answered the phone?

Snehlata pressed his head; was he having a headache? He shook his head, no he was just tired, no headache.

* * *

No headache, but the heartache continued for Ramesh Patnaik through Saturday. He was depressed, it showed on his sad face like the aftereffects of the painful sting of a bee. On Sunday morning Snehlata insisted on going for a movie, Pyar Kaa Side Effects. The kids refused, their friends would make fun of them for weeks, these days which kid accompanies parents for movies? The owner of Swati Talkies was Snehlata's classmate in college. She called him and asked for two passes for the box office for the afternoon show.

Ramesh Patnaik went to the movie just for a little distraction. It was not a bad movie. He started enjoying it. In the interval lights came up and people started going out for snacks and drinks. The manager sent a boy with soft drink and popcorn. Ramesh Patnaik had got up and started stretching his arm and legs. Snehlata nudged him, "I wish our daughter Sharanya had come with us. Look at the father daughter duo there in the balcony, how she is holding his hand and they are going out for their drink and snacks."

Ramesh Patnaik looked, and the next moment his heart stopped; he sat down, shocked. Banamali Garabadu and Anima! Ye God, is there any fair play in your scheme of things? For the last one month Ramesh Patnaik was a moth dancing like mad, desperately trying to fall into the flame, and the flame chooses to jump into a bucket of ice! What magic did Banamali play on her? The hall became dark, as dark as his heart. He got up and told Snehlata he wanted to go home, he was having a splitting headache. As they walked out, he wished he could ask the old wizard on Monday to share the secret of his trick with him!

GLOSSARY

Arey Pagli – You crazy girl

Bhaina – Elder brother

Bindi – The dot applied on the forehead by ladies

Pakoda, Kebab, Tikka – Tasty snacks items

Pranam, Sashtang Pranam – Salute, salute from the ground

Saree – The long, colourful cloth used by ladies to drape their body

THE OLD FOX

"**W**here is the old fox today? Not seen so far!"

Vinita, my friend, gave me a big nudge and laughed loudly.

"I don't know. May be he is out of town." I replied.

"Yeah, I can see your restlessness for the past half an hour. Don't tell me you are missing him?"

"Of course not, what a preposterous idea!"

"But something is wrong Ranju, tell me what it is."

"Actually, I am missing the way his eyes sparkle like a flashlight when he sees us."

Vinita gave me another nudge and rolled with laughter. Vinita and I had been friends for the past twelve years. We were in school together. When we passed out of high school this summer, she went to the co-educational BJB College and I joined Ramadevi Women's College. She insisted on going to a co-educational college ("There is no fun yaar, if you don't have boys looking at you, like they are going to eat you up!"). My grandma didn't allow me to go to BJB, so I had to be in an all-girls college. For the first time Vinita and I were separated. Throughout our school years we had eaten from the same lunch box, giggled over the same jokes and read the same novels in class away from the stern gaze of the teachers.

For the past three months we had been meeting at the park every morning. Usually we took five rounds of the park. Vinita loved to talk and was a real chatter-box. We caught up on a lot of issues, her college, my college, and the friends we had made. Vinita was quite a stunner in looks and loved to display her figure. Just three months into the college, she had managed to step into the sweet world of love and courtship with a prince charming, who was relentlessly pursuing her with mind-blowing devotion. These days she kept talking about her hero all the time, how he waited outside when her classes ended, how they stood under the tree chatting for hours. Sometimes her mobile phone would ring in the morning during our walk, and she would get lost in her hero's world, completely ignoring me!

Compared to Vinita, I was a plain-looking girl, although my grandma used to say that my eyes were captivating, and could melt even a statue. I lost my mother at the time of my birth. Baba never married again, he was deeply in love with my mother. I rarely heard him talk about her but on different occasions I had seen him sitting before her photograph and gazing at her in a pensive way. The day he got a promotion last year from section officer to under-secretary, he kept telling grandma, "Manju would have been so happy today."

My grandma was the centre of our lives and everything revolved around her. She ran our lives and no one questioned her authority. Baba usually took us to a movie every weekend and we would go for dinner at a restaurant afterwards. This was the routine for us for a long time, rarely deviated.

And the old fox? He was an elderly man, who had been coming to the park for the past one month. From his looks and manners he seemed to be a senior government official. I had seen a few officers while moving with Baba. On some of the weekends while having dinner Baba would point out to us the elderly gentleman sitting with his family at the corner table, "Look, that is Basu sahab, the Transport Secretary". If Basu sahab's gaze fell on Baba, he would stand up and greet him. Basu sahib would nod his head and continue eating.

One evening Baba's boss came to the restaurant when we were having dinner. Our table was close to the entrance and he saw Baba the moment he entered. There was a slight hint of annoyance, but he hid it instantly. Baba got up and nudged me also to stand up and greet his boss. Mahanty babu, Baba's boss looked at me and said,

"Arabinda, this is your daughter?"

"Yes sir, she is Ranjana, my daughter. She is a student at the Unit Six Girls' School."

"Good. She is a pretty girl! You should bring her home sometime. This is Monica, my niece from Delhi."

Baba's boss tried to charm me with an oily smile and moved on to another table. As soon as he was out of our hearing range, I asked,

"Baba, how is it his niece didn't even greet us and didn't say a word?"

Baba didn't answer but suddenly grandma broke into a big, loud laugh, like she had gone crazy or something. Baba felt embarrassed and tried to hush her up.

"Maa, don't laugh so loud. People are looking at us!"

"Aru, you were telling me the other day that your boss goes to the restaurant with a new niece every week! Why don't you tell that to Ranju?"

Baba kept mum and threw a sharp look at her. I felt shy. My grandma was quite an item! Did a father say such things to his school-going daughter? Anyway, our dinner that evening became a disaster, with the unwanted intrusion of his boss into our talk.

Like me and Vinny, the old man had been a regular in the park every morning. The first time he saw us he glanced away and kept on walking. But gradually we noticed that every time he passed us from the opposite direction, he would slow down, cast a lingering look at us and move on. He also made it a point to arrive at the park at the same time as us and walk for five rounds in the opposite direction. So he would pass us ten times during the walk and his eyes would be fixed on us while we cross his path.

First I thought he must be looking at Vinny, because she was an absolute knock-out, and wore tight-fitting dresses which revealed the contours of her body in a suggestive way. So I complimented Vinny,

"So, Vinny! Sixteen to sixty, boys to men, everyone is a victim of your looks! Lucky you!"

Vinita was hugely pleased. "I am like that, one in a million!"

But next time uncle passed us, Vinny gave me a big nudge and said,

"Hey, Ranju, did you mark? He is not looking at me, he directs his full gaze on you. And guess what? It's a funny look, like he is going to eat you up! My God, the old fox, still trying to catch a young chick?"

I didn't believe her, for two reasons. First, with Vinny by my side, why should anyone look at me? Second, he was fairly old, must be fifty three, or fifty four.

I gave a push to Vinita.

"Get lost, you vamp, you have a dirty mind. That uncle must be fifty three, fifty four years old. Why are you reading so much into his glance?"

"Ranju yaar, fifty-three, love is free, fifty-four, wife is a bore. Don't you remember how our classmate Sheila's uncle ran away with his typist to Gopalpur beach and raised such a stink in the town last year? He was fifty four. So love and lust know no age. Isn't it Shakespeare who said that?"

Vinita looked pleased with this priceless nugget plucked from God knows where!

"No, not Shakespeare, it is your dirty-mind, Vinny dear, which invented it! You have a way of putting dirty thoughts into everything. It must be your overflowing libido oozing through your tight dress! For all that you know this uncle may be a decent man."

"Decent, my foot! If he is decent, he should be looking at your face, why is he giving you that hungry, sweeping look from your head to toe! I am telling you, he is an old fox, just licking his lips in anticipation of a good meal."

That's how the uncle came to be called the 'old fox' by Vinny, every time she spoke about him. I was quite shy by nature, thanks to the long lecture my grandma gave me about chastity and the poison that was supposed to be spewing when boys cast their glance at me. In fact, if one took my grandma seriously, even those glances had the power to make a girl pregnant! Compared to Vinny's depth of knowledge about love and sex I was like that famous scientist who felt like he was collecting pebbles on the shore when the vast ocean of knowledge lay unexplored before him.

So next time the uncle passed us, I stole a brief glance at him and a shiver ran down my back. I got puzzled by his searching look, directed exclusively at me, completely ignoring Vinita. It was a peculiar, hungry kind of look, as if inviting me to come near him and to accept his offer of friendship. Being a student of psychology, I knew that face was the index of mind. From his intense looks and the flushed face, I had no doubt about his intentions. Vinny saw the puzzled look in my face and burst out laughing,

"Idiot, go and tell your grandma, how she has failed in her mission. She sent you to a Women's college to keep you away from the boys and now an old man has fallen for you! I pity you Ranju! An old man, who looks like an old fox! Such bad luck! What will you do with him? Except wash his dirty underwear?"

I felt annoyed with Vinny. Why was she dragging the matter so far? Dirty underwear? Ugh! Disgusting! Vinny really had a sick mind!

"Hey, Vinny, looks like everything dirty appeals to your sick mind. Dirty underwear? Can't you think of anything better from that uncle?"

Vinita broke into an earth-shaking guffaw. It was her special day of pulling my legs and teasing me to death!

"So, you get those piercing looks from Old Fox, and you have started having kind thoughts about him? Ranju,

Ranju, beware of old foxes, they have long teeth and sharp claws!"

"Vinny, you are being unduly harsh on him. How do you know what is in his mind?"

"So, you have become a mind reader? Tell me what is in his mind? Trust me Ranju; I am more experienced than you! Anyway I will consult my hero today about the old fox and tell you tomorrow,"

From next day we took special care to guess what was in the uncle's mind. Vinita's hero threw up his hands, saying he had no time to think of old foxes when his mind thought of nothing other than her, all the time. He felt twenty four hours did not give him enough time to dream about her. So, there was no space in his mind for old foxes. From the behaviour of the uncle, we had no doubt that he was eager to come closer to us and perhaps to befriend me. There was no question of my going anywhere near him. Every time he passed by, my heartbeats would increase, as if the sounds of a mild drum were reverberating in my heart. I would quicken my pace, leaving Vinny a little surprised.

Looking at my uneasiness, Vinny suggested that we could avoid the old fox by going to the adjacent park, though it was much smaller and not so well-maintained. It would be at least a relief from the unwanted gaze of the old pervert. We did that, but after two days he was with us walking in the smaller park, a hurt look on his face, silently asking us, how we could ditch him. We knew there was no escape from him! So we resumed our walk in the main park.

One day while walking I twisted my ankle. Groaning in pain, I dragged myself to a bench with the help of Vinny and sat down. From there we could see the uncle feeling bewildered, looking here and there. His face darkened, he was lost in thought and moved on. In the next round he spotted us and his face lit up, like a lost child finding its mother. He took his walk very close to us, looking at me in a questioning way as if asking, "What happened? Why did you sit down? Get up, let's continue the walk. Let's talk to each other with our eyes. Why aren't you getting up?"

Uncle didn't stop. He had just slowed down. We looked helplessly at him and he left. He was probably getting late for the office. When I came home limping, an arm over Vinita's shoulder, Baba got scared. I tried to convince him that it was just a twisting of the ankle, but he immediately called his office and applied for a day's leave. I chided him,

"Baba, you will unnecessarily get into problem with your boss. As it is, he is a difficult man to please."

Baba smiled indulgently and shook his head.

"No way! I am not going to office today, when you are sick. And didn't I mention to you, I have had a change of boss recently? The new man is a gem of a person and is exactly the opposite of Mahanty Sir. There was so much tension in the office earlier - Mahanty Sir was never satisfied with anybody's work, he used to shout at people and often threw files at them. He would go away for lunch with clients, take drinks and return to office around four. In the evenings he would go to a restaurant or to Bhubaneswar Club to consume liquor again. Sometimes he would assign work to people before leaving and people had to sit late in the office to finish the work. The new boss, Mr. Tripathy is a saintly person, soft-spoken and mild-mannered. He never shouts at people and leaves office promptly at six. He asks everyone to go home early to spend time with their family. 'Anyone who works beyond six in office must be cheating during daytime', that's what he says. Tripathy Sir is an excellent team leader and trusts his sub-ordinates. The other day he called me and said, 'Arabinda Babu, I am giving you this sensitive file. You must deal with it yourself. Please don't pass it down. Analyse the issue properly, whatever you write I will accept, but try to be objective.' Tell me Ranju, isn't it nice to work for a boss like him?"

I nodded. I was happy that Baba had got a good boss at office.

When Vinita turned up for walk next morning, I couldn't accompany her because of the sprained ankle. She hesitated, but I pushed her, "Go and watch uncle's reaction when he doesn't see me."

Vinita looked at me and burst out laughing.

"Oh, the matter has gone this far! The young chick is pining for the old fox! Looks like you are sunk. Poor Ranju, what bad luck! You should have come to my college yaar; at least some love-lorn teenager would have swept you off your feet. But look at your luck! This wretched old fox has won your heart! You are getting restless if you don't see him! What a pity! What a miserable pity! I am really disgusted with you."

She started leaving for the park and I hollered after her, "Vinny, go and speak to uncle, tell him I am going to fix him with my grandma!" She threw another disgusting look at me and ran away.

She returned after one hour, excited,

"Hey Ranju, looks like the old fox will go crazy if he doesn't see you tomorrow. Today he went pale when he saw me alone! Kept looking at me every time we passed, I thought he would stop me and enquire about you. But he didn't have the courage, I guess. I look like a cracker about to burst, you know. One day when I am not there, he will pounce on you."

"Why do you say like that? May be, he is not such a bad fellow?"

"Oh oh! So, he is not bad, only I am bad, is it? OK, I will come here only when you recover. I don't want to be mauled by the old fox!" Vinita left in mock anger.

We resumed our walk after three days. Uncle's face showed a big relief when he saw me. In fact he broke into a huge grin and there was a fresh bounce in his walk that day. Vinita had a great laugh.

"The old fox is besotted with the young chick! Look at him, smiling away like a coy lover! What a waste of your life, Ranju! If you really want to have a lover pine away for you, change your college, come to mine. At least I can fix a teenager for you!"

I kept quiet. I still didn't know why uncle was obsessed with me.

Meanwhile, three months passed since we first saw the uncle taking a walk in the park. During the pooja holidays Vinita had to go to Rourkela, along with her mother. Her grandfather was seriously ill, on the verge of collapsing any time. Vinita was initially not keen on going, but her hero said he would be also coming to Rourkela to spend the holidays with his elder brother. Then Vinita got terribly excited.

"It's going to be great fun yaar. I will go and watch a movie with my hero and we will eat ice cream during the interval, licking it from the same cone" – the last statement delivered with emphasis, looking at me in an arching way, designed to make me feel deficient in the matter of love.

When I said nothing, she was annoyed, "Ok, I will return early, you stay away from the old fox. I don't want to see his teeth marks and claw scratches on you when I come back!"

The next morning when uncle saw me alone, his face lit up. I thought I saw a twinkle in his eyes. Every time he passed me, I imagined he tried to come a little closer. After three rounds I felt uneasy and left the park for home.

I had decided that I would not go to the park again till Vinita came back, but the next day I got up early and felt restless sitting at home. So I went to the park. Uncle's face brightened up on seeing me. When he passed me during the second round, he came very close to me and asked, "What is the time?" My heart stopped for a few seconds. Sweat appeared on my face and my legs trembled. I lifted my hand, shook my head and showed him my bare wrist. I ran away from the park and till I reached home, my heart was thumping. I finally decided not to come to the park till Vinita returned.

The next morning I told Grandma that I didn't feel like going to the park alone in the absence of Vinita. She asked my father to accompany me. Baba agreed immediately. He had not been to a park for a long time. From an old trunk he took out a pair of stylish sunglasses and a white fur cap, put them on and moved out. I put my foot down.

"Baba, there is no way I am coming with you, if you put on those two ghastly objects. I don't want you to look like a Tamil hero if you want to walk with me."

Baba immediately agreed to discard the fur cap and the sunglasses. He was really excited to come with me to the park, like a child going to a circus. When we reached the park, he kept on asking me, how many rounds I took, how much time it took to complete one round, whether I was ready to compete with him in one round of walk. I laughed at his excitement, but I was getting increasingly nervous. What would happen when we came close to uncle? If he looked at me in that typically hungry way, how would Baba react? What a shame! What would Baba think of me, if uncle tried to speak to me again? And what if Baba picked up a fight with him? But then I tried to reassure myself, hoping uncle would not be so stupid, trying to talk to me when Baba was with me.

I became aware that Baba had repeated his question and was looking curiously at me, wondering why I was lost in thought. I replied,

"Baba, how do I know how much time it takes to complete one round in the park? You haven't given me a watch, nor do I have a mobile phone."

"Am I such a bad father? You have so many complaints against me?" Baba asked in mock despair.

I laughed. I loved my Baba too much to have any complaints against him.

"Sorry Baba, don't take it to heart. I was only joking. I don't need a watch, nor a mobile phone. But will you buy me a treadmill? Then I don't have to come to the park alone to take a walk. It is really frightening to walk alone here."

Baba stopped and looked at me, alarmed.

"Why are you saying that? Tell me, is anybody harassing you here? No doubt I have stopped going to the Gym. But even now I have enough force in my punches to knock out the teeth of any ruffian."

I was happy, making an imaginary connection between Uncle's teeth and Baba's swinging fist. I thought I would tell Baba the cause of my nervousness.

"Actually Baba.............

Baba picked up my hand and stopped me. I saw uncle a few feet from us. He had appeared from nowhere, emerging out of the shadow of a huge banyan tree. Baba went forward, bowed his head and did a huge Namaskar to him,

"Sir, so nice to see you. Do you come here every morning?"

Seeing Baba, Uncle's face beamed with pleasure,

"Arey, Arabinda babu. Such a pleasure to see you. We are meeting in the park for the first time!"

I stood there transfixed. So the uncle, the old fox, was known to Baba! Baba came to me. And holding my hand, virtually dragged me to the Uncle.

"Say Namaskar to my boss! I have told you what a great man he is, a God-like person."

My heart started beating violently. God-like person, this uncle? Then how about the man who harassed me every day by those suggestive looks and the unwelcome attempts to speak to me? Was this man a split personality?

But I obeyed Baba and went forward to wish him. His face lit up.

"Arabinda Babu, this is your daughter! How nice! I see her in this park every day. What's your name? And where is your friend? Why she is not coming for the past two days?"

"Uncle, my name is Ranjana and my friend's name is Vinita. She has gone to Rourkela to see her ailing grandfather. I was just now telling Baba that he should buy me a treadmill so that I don't have to come to the park alone to take a walk."

I deliberately said this to remind him of his boorish behaviour and how I disliked it. Uncle's face became pale. But then, he composed himself.

"Arabinda babu, Ranjana is a very sweet girl. I will gift her a treadmill on her birthday."

Baba almost fainted in panic, thinking of such a costly gift from his boss.....

"No, no, sir, why should you buy such a costly gift for Ranjana? I will buy it for her."

"Not at all. You won't understand Arabinda babu, it's a very small price to pay to get the love of a sweet girl like Ranjana."

I was startled. Love? A treadmill to win my love? So finally the cat was out of the bag!

"Actually Arabinda babu, I have a daughter named Laali, who is studying in the US for the past four years. My wife has also gone there for the last six months. I love my daughter too much and miss her all the time. Ranjana looks exactly like my Laali, same height, same colour. Every day when I look at Ranjana I feel that if she was a bit fatter, she and Laali would be looking like twin sisters!"

I felt like someone had passed an electric current through me. The shock was terrible. I missed Vinita. If she was with me, I would have given her a big slap. The rascal had such a dirty mind! I bowed my head in shame and told uncle,

"Thank you, uncle, for such affectionate thoughts. I will come to the park every day to give you company. We will chat about Laali."

Baba was relieved. He was still perturbed by the thought of his boss buying a costly gift for me.

"So sir, in that case you need not buy a treadmill for Ranju."

Uncle and I laughed out loud. In a taunting tone I said,

"But uncle, you should buy me a watch so that if you ask what time it is, I will be able to tell you!"

Uncle let out a loud laugh.

"That's a perfect timing! To fish for a gift!"

Baba gave me a hard, intimidating look. But I didn't care. Now that baba's boss was on my side, I acted kind of cool!

GLOSSARY

Yaar – A form of addressing a friend

Arey – A form of addressing a friend or an acquaintance

Uncle – A form of addressing an elder acquaintance

– 8 –

THE STALKER

Unlike other days Abdul Mian woke up as late as nine this morning. His eyelids were heavy, the face a mask of deep worries when he came up and stood near the door waiting for his cup of tea. Ruksana saw her husband from the kitchen and came running.

"What happened today? Don't you have to go to work this morning? I have been waiting since six o' clock with your tea and breakfast. I have packed your lunch also. How come you kept on sleeping?"

Abdul just shook his head,

"Don't feel like going to work today. I have a splitting headache."

Ruksana's face darkened,

"Hai Allah! That's why you were tossing restlessly last night. I heard some whimpering and some incoherent words. Once you also cried out in pain. I tried to wake you up, but you just turned over and kept sleeping. What happened to you? Did you have a bad dream?"

Abdul winced at her words. Bad dream? Yes, he had a bad dream last night. Except that it was not a dream, it happened with him in the darkness of the road abutting the maidan.

On the way to his basti. Last night a little after nine. In a matter of few minutes, a man had turned into a monster.

Ruksana touched his forehead with her work-worn calloused hands. There was no fever. Yet Abdul was sweating like a feverish man in this cold November morning. The poor chap must be ill, otherwise who sweats like this on a winter morning?

Ruksana had warmed up his tea by now and handed it to him. He looked at his wife,

"Where is Zeenat? Has she left for college?"

"No, she is taking a bath. Her friend Ameena is coming in ten minutes. Ameena has to take the bus to college today. It seems her scooty broke down last evening in the market."

Abdul had lifted the cup for a sip of the tea. For a moment it remained frozen in mid-air. His heart started pounding. He turned back to his room and wearily lowered himself to the bed. Ameena is coming in a few minutes! Does she know Abdul is at home? What if................

The pounding of Abdul's heart almost sounded like the thumping of the lathe machine in the factory where he worked. Like it had done a hundred times after he returned home, his mind went back to last night. A dark night, turned muggy with intermittent drizzles. Abdul had got down from the bus and started walking for home in his basti half a kilometre away. The road was deserted. Almost all the street lights were out.

Abdul saw someone walking a few steps ahead of him. He peered into the darkness and could make out it was a lady with a burkha draped on her. A lady! At this time of the night?

She was almost running. The dark night, the lonely road and the slight drizzle must have put some fear in her. Abdul quickened his pace. He looked at her from behind, a sudden hunger rising deep in his stomach - a primordial hunger which knows no conscience and is unfettered by any qualms. For a moment he tried to guess if the woman was young or old, but decided it didn't matter. Her walk was swift and lively, probably a young girl hurrying home. The hunger in his body grew, a silent growl seizing him like a coiling rope out to choke him in an insane desire.

Abdul started creeping up quickly, but silently. The woman should not know she was being followed. She had looked back only once, but luckily Abdul was under a thick tree at the time and she could not see him.

A dark night, a deserted road, a slight, shivering cold, and a frightened, lonely woman - what else one needs to warm up the night with some hot pleasure? For a fleeting moment he thought of his frustration at home - Ruksana was no longer the desirable woman she used to be, and for the last couple of years she had spurned his advances all the time, reminding him of the grown up daughter of marriageable age at home.

"Tobah, Tobah, what will Zeenat think if she gets the slightest hint of your insatiable appetite? Her Abba is a lecherous old man? Chhi Chhi, control yourself Zeenat ke Abba! Do your Namaz and read Quran for two hours every day."

Namaz? Of course he did his Namaz five times a day, but at night his frustration became unbearable. Abdul tried to remember when was the last he had touched a woman's body. May be three months back. He had gone to the red light area one evening on the way back from office. But the woman who had charged him two hundred rupees for half an hour was not even worth a fifty. She had just lain on the dirty bed like a corpse when Abdul was humping all his passions into her. It was all over in ten minutes and she had kicked him out.

Abdul remained frustrated, the invisible hunger gnawing at his body all the time. The few women at the packing section in the factory flirted with him once in a while, but whenever he made a pass at anyone of them, they would roll in laughter, leaving him more frustrated and in nagging humiliation.

Abdul shivered with anticipation. Tonight he will not be kicked out. The woman under the burkha would be at his command once he dragged her into a bench in the park. She would do whatever he wanted her to do. Abdul was only a few steps behind her now. Looked like a slim body, probably a young woman, he thought. Ah, let this be a night of intense pleasure, a compensation for months of frustration and deprivation!

Abdul looked to all sides. Nobody was in sight. The area outside the maidan was dark; the lights at the entrance were not working, thanks to the incompetence of the municipal staff of the small town. A slight drizzle had started falling. The night was getting colder.

With stealthy footsteps he came behind the woman. She must have sensed his presence. She tried to turn but Abdul gave her no chance. He pounced on her; put a hand on her mouth ad gripped her firmly. She started exerting to escape, but Abdul was too strong for her.

He started dragging her towards the entrance of the maidan. The body was light, and slim. Abdul's excitement was growing.

Suddenly he stumbled on the broken pavement near the entrance and his foot slipped. But he kept a firm grip on the woman. For a moment his hand slipped from her mouth and she started screaming,

"Please leave me, let me go, in the name of Allah have mercy on me".

Suddenly Abdul stood still! The voice sounded familiar! Is it someone he knew? Seizing the brief interlude of dilemma the girl looked back at the precise moment when there was a big lightning, the first lightning of the evening. She saw his face and shrieked,

"Chachajaan, I am Ameena, please let me go, please!"

Abdul winced as if a snake from the maidan had bitten his leg. Ameena? His daughter Zeenat's friend, who lived in the same street five houses away! Ya Allah!

Abdul's grip loosened and before he could recover, Ameena freed herself and ran away into the dark night towards their basti.

Abdul sat down on the pavement leading to the gate of the maidan. His mind was in turmoil. Ya Allah, what did he do? How could he fall so low? How would he show his face to Ruksana and Zeenat when Ameena told them about this?

His head bent with worry, Abdul came home at midnight. Ruksana was waiting for him with dinner. He just shook his head and went to the bathroom to change his soggy dress. When he came to bed, sleep eluded him. In the longest night of his life, he tossed and turned and had recurring nightmares. Once he saw Zeenat falling at his feet and begging him, Abba, let me go, please leave me. Another time he saw in his dreams a police man coming to his house and arresting him, telling everyone, this old man is a pervert, a criminal, and Ruksana falling at the policeman's feet, saying, do whatever you want with me but please spare him. Every time Abdul closed his eyes, Ameena's shriek came back to haunt him - *Chachajaan, I am Ameena, please let me go, in Allah's name, please.* He would get up as if an electric current had passed through him. He desperately wanted to drink a glass of water but his limbs felt lifeless, refusing to carry him to the kitchen.

Remembering all these dreams brought tears to Abdul's eyes. Will Allah forgive him?

Abdul woke up from his reverie. Bits of conversation were wafting from the entrance room. Ameena must have come! Abdul broke into a sweat. He started shivering. His throat felt constricted as if a big ball had got stuck there. With leaden feet he dragged himself to the connecting door and stood there. Ruksana and Zeenat were sitting at the small dining table facing the main entrance door, with their back to Abdul's room. They could not see him standing at the door. But Ameena could, she was facing the connecting door.

Ruksana was asking Ameena,

"Hai Allah, how could you leave your scooty in the market? What if somebody steals it?"

"Chachijaan, how can someone steal the scooty? It refuses to start!"

Zeenat looked at her,

"So you came by bus from the market?"

"Yes, but you know what happened to me when I was walking down from the bus stop? I had the most horrible experience of my life. You won't believe if I tell you!"

Zeenat could not wait to hear what was the most horrible experience of her friend.

"What happened?"

Suddenly Ameena's eyes were drawn to a slight movement at the connecting door. Abdul Mian was standing there, like a forlorn, fallen ghost, with tears in his eyes and hands folded in a prayer for mercy.

It was just a fleeting glance, lasting fraction of a second and Ameena continued her tale.

"It was dark last night; almost all the street lights were out. The roads were deserted, thanks to the drizzle. I was scared, walking alone. Near the gate of the maidan someone pounced on me from behind. I almost died at the spot. I wanted to shout for help, but could not. The man held me in a tight grip and closed my mouth with his hand......."

Ruksana jumped up,

"What? What are you saying?"

"Yes, Chachijaan, I felt as if my limbs were going limp. He started dragging me towards the park"

"Hai Allah, what kind of sick people are there, jumping on a young girl?"

"Chachijaan, I was in a burkha, he had no way of knowing whether it was a young girl or an old woman under the burkha"

Zeenat shouted,

"Even then the pervert had no business to pounce on you. How did you escape?"

"He stumbled on the pavement near the gate and I freed myself. I kept running till I reached home. I was so scared; I was shivering on the bed throughout the night. My Abbu had already gone to sleep, and you know Ammijaan has gone to Khala's place. I felt shy to tell Abbu; Anyway he would have scolded me for going to the market in the evening. So I am waiting for Ammijaan to return tomorrow. I will tell her".

Zeenat was seething with anger,

"What kind of horrible demon would do a despicable thing like that? Was he someone from our basti? Did you see his face?"

Ameena shook her head, with a deliberate, painful slowness.

"No, I told you it was pitch dark. I could not see his face."

"So, what are you going to do? Will you file a complaint with the police? May be the wretch had also got down from a bus and was following you. The police will find out in no time. He should be caught and sent to jail."

Ameena sat with her head bent for a few seconds, then she looked up. There was no anger in her eyes, only the hint of an infinite sadness.

"You know last night when I was shivering on bed out of fear, I was thinking on that line, but now I have changed my mind."

"Changed your mind? Are you crazy?"- Zeenat shrieked.

Ameena shook her head,

"No, I am not crazy. May be the man has a family to support and his going to jail will devastate them. May be at this moment he is standing somewhere, with tears in his eyes and with folded hands begging for mercy and forgiveness. I want to give him a chance to reform."

Before a stunned Zeenat could recover, Ameena got up,

"Come, let's leave. We are getting late. With some luck we will still be able to catch the college bus".

GLOSSARY

Abba/ Abbu – Father

Ammi – Mother

Basti – A settlement of people, usually from economically backward class

Burkha – The black drape Muslim women use to cover their body while going out

Chaachajaan/Chaachiijaan – Uncle/Aunty

Khalaa – Father's sister

Maidan – Park

Namaz – Prayer offered by Muslims five times every day

– 9 –

AFTERNOON RAINS

"**A**re you crazy? You walked all the way drenched in these rains?"

"You know how I love the rains, looking at the sky, feeling the rain drops on my face. How I adore the way they soak me and churn my heart……Moreover, I didn't find the umbrellas. I don't know where Rajani kept them before leaving for Singapore to be with our daughter".

"I am also alone at home. Anandini has gone to Bangalore to help her ailing brother's family. As if being old is not enough, we have to bear the pangs of loneliness also. That, my friend, is our destiny".

"Lonely? You think you are lonely? With this big lawn, the green, wet grass, the gently swaying flowers, this riot of colours! With all this how can you be lonely? You want to know what loneliness is, ask me! Being in a small three bedroom apartment, dirty, grimy walls outside the window, another nameless, joyless flat when you open the door, mangled electric wires and dry branches of decrepit trees overlooking the balcony-confined to that my friend, is loneliness."

"Do you want to come in, or keep soaking in the rains? But let me warn you, I can't offer you even a cup of tea. The maid won't come before six and it's only three in the afternoon.

Maids in Delhi, as you know, work like machines, their timings are precise, clock like!"

"I know my friend, you think I have come here to have tea? I have come to stand on your green lawn and get soaked in rain. I want to look at the yellow, orange, white, flowers, keep seeing them till they become a part of my memory like a painting on a wall. I want to close my eyes and touch their smiling petals, feel the throb of their soft hearts. I want the rain drops to soak my heart and spread their colour all over my consciousness. When I open my eyes, I want to see colours everywhere, the sky, the earth, the rains, on you, on me and on my memory."

"In your memory? What memory? You are in a terrific mood today! Is it the effect of the rains? Or of the vacant Sunday afternoon in a soulless Delhi? You know, I am a serious sort of person, spent my whole life pouring over government files. Unlike you, a professor spending time with young hearts year after year, I don't understand many of these delicate matters of colours, throb of hearts in soft petals and rain drops soaking the heart."

"My friend, my idiot friend, these are not things to be understood, they are to be felt, felt with every breath you inhale."

"Oh! Felt with every breath? How do you do that?"

"Feel something? So easy! See, I am looking at you, talking to you, but you know, my mind is actually somewhere else, it has gone back to many years, feeling some presence, in my heart, in my subconscious mind. That feeling is different from what I am seeing before me. What I feel is deep within, a soft glow lighting up my soul, like a soft light hiding shyly in a corner of a room. When that feeling engulfs you, it brings mild goosebumps on you, a soft voice brings you many memories, many images. They whisper to you, don't you remember me, have I become a stranger to you, no longer a part of your consciousness! A feeling is like a shadow playing hide and seek with you, one moment you feel it intensely, the next moment it disappears leaving an aching melancholy in you. It is something that you experience when you see a good painting, read a good poem or listen to a good song."

"You are getting more and more philosophical! Come inside, you are completely drenched, you may fall sick."

"A little more rains will do no harm. Let me feel your lawn a little longer, and touch the beautiful flowers some more. God knows when Delhi will have rains like this again, a Sunday afternoon getting soaked in dripping rain, the soft glow of the sun drooping behind serious looking clouds and flowers laughing their hearts out at this primordial game. And me standing near the flowers, tormented by some long past memory, trying to touch it!"

"My God, what has happened to you? It seems the dripping rains and a bed of flowers have driven you crazy, where are you lost? What memory? Whose memory?"

"Bring two umbrellas, come out from your portico, let's go to the flower bed. I will show you how to feel the flowers"

....

"Ok, here we are. Now tell me what you feel in the flowers, which I don't."

"Look at this white dahlia, what do you see in its petals?"

"Are you kidding me? What I see in the petals? They are just white petals!"

"Close your eyes, think of those petals and remember the most beautiful girl in your college clad in a white saree, remember a white night of splendid moonlight falling like a cascading waterfall, think of the white clouds of an autumn sky, or the wild foams of breaking waves, the snow clad mountains looking benignly at you………And then touch the petals. Are you not able to feel them?"

"Yes, I can think of them when you told me, but tell me how do you see so many things in such a small piece of petal?"

"If you try only to see them, you won't know what is hidden in them. Try to feel them in your mind. Haven't you ever seen a beautiful tree-canopied street, a nice building against pale street lights, a smiling moon behind doting clouds, a cute small girl laughing, and thought of capturing them in your mind's camera so that they are stored there forever? That is the power of felling something, not merely seeing it."

"What else you feel in these flowers? What about those thin yellow lines in the white flowers?"

"That is how nature tells us she is the best artist in the world. See the blue streaks in the violet flower - which painter would ever think of combining these two colours to make it so maddeningly beautiful? Look at the deep red singaneria - doesn't it remind you of a burning cinder, a full bloomed rose, the vermillion on a goddess's forehead, the red bangles of a bride, or a swarm of beatles on the grass? Close your eyes, feel the colour, all these will become alive in your mind."

"Enough, enough my friend, let's go inside, the rains are getting heavier………………Take this towel, wipe yourself and put on these dry clothes. You are one hell of a crazy fellow, otherwise who wants to get wet like this?"

"Why do you look at rains as rains? Don't they mean anything else to you?"

"O my God, what has come over you? Rains are rains! What else can they mean?"

"No my friend, rains are not mere drops of water falling from the sky, they are cascades of memory, drops of tears from some wet eyes from the past. I came to your lawn to look at these green lawns, the coloured flowers and relive those memories, to collect those tears in my palms and wash away some traces of guilt."

"What guilt, what are you saying?"

"The silent fire that is smouldering in me for years. An abandoned milestone whose shadow lengthens with every advancing step in my life's walk."

"Looks like you are missing Rajani too much, the vibrant Rajani, the walking combination of Amrita Pritam and Simone de Beauvoir. You are so lucky, my friend to have an intellectual wife!"

"Intellectual? What do I do with an intellectual wife, who doesn't even remember any longer how to share a smile, a laugh with me! Have you ever seen her room? There are used plates, mugs, saucers everywhere, books upon books piled on the floor, on her bed, her table. If I don't clean up her room, she will have to jump over books or climb on them to reach her bed."

"What do you mean her room, her bed? Is your room different from hers?"

"Yes, for so many years we have been living under the same roof, but only as flat mates. She runs away to her daughter whenever she can. I am too non-intellectual for the mother and the daughter, too rustic, too pedestrian. But can you imagine, when we first met we couldn't live without each other even for a day?"

"That's why you got married, didn't you? Two love birds building an early nest! ....What? Are you leaving? Come, I will see you off at the gate. Take one of these umbrellas with you, don't get wet again."

"No, no umbrella, didn't I tell you, how much I like to get wet in the rains, it's like getting soaked in a tormenting memory, a memory that has haunted me for the last forty one years".

"What memory? Whose memory? What had happened forty one years back to torment you for so long?"

"Forty one years back, I was a twenty year old, she, my love, was seventeen. It was a rainy afternoon, like this, the sun was playing hide and seek with clouds, we stood near a flower bed in Forest Park in Bhubaneswar. I held her hand, looked into her eyes, and told her, 'look at these flowers, remember their colour, one day I will buy a saree for you to match each of these colours.'"

"Oh, I didn't know you were so romantic, at least not in the school where we studied! Who was the girl?"

"She used to live five houses away in the same street in the government colony at Unit six. She herself was like a flower, soft, delicate and innocent. A year later we walked to the Park, soaked in rain, the lawns were green, the grass was wet. There was a bed of flowers in a corner which was a riot of colours, our hearts were wet with tears, the impending separation was tearing them to pieces. I was to leave for JNU the next day, to join my MA course. I told her, 'Keep this day locked in your mind. One day I will bring you here and remind you how I had left my heart with you, how much I loved you.' She just shook her head, 'You will forget me, like everyone does.' And then she started crying. I had no words to console her, I was myself in tears."

"What happened, how did you get hooked to Rajani?"

"JNU was a different world altogether, for someone coming from a small town like Bhubaneswar it was a magical world, a world of excitement and romance. Within a few months there was hardly anyone who was not hooked to someone or the other. I fell for Rajani like a ton of bricks tumbling from a wayward truck. She was so slim, so smart, when she walked in her short skirt and top, she looked like a school girl who had lost her way into a university. Her father was a big officer in Kerala. The way she spoke English was mesmerising, she quoted Shakespeare, Keats and Eliot like they were her cousins, and she smoked, she drank like a fish, she danced, when she walked it was like a young, lovely deer in search of her soul mate."

"My God! Yes, I can imagine that, she must have been a livewire. How did she fall for you, a country bumpkin?"

"She didn't fall for me, she adopted me, as her little lamb. She told everyone I was her pet, and I felt I was probably the luckiest pet in the world. JNU in those initial years was a hot bed of revolutionary, nonconformist ideas and she wanted to prove herself to be the champion nonconformist. So she spurned the advances of many elitist snobs and chose the most simple, shy student in the class as her pet. I tried to transform myself, I started smoking with her, cigarette, pot and then we went unto LSD, we drank beer from the same bottle, and we danced together, she like a little fairy and I like a primitive tribal. Our tango echoed in the campus, like the animal grunts of many other young couples. To show her daring, nonconformist nature, she was one of the first girls to move into the men's hostel and in my single bedded room we discovered the passion of life with hungry abandon."

"Lucky you, the taste of the forbidden fruit so early in life!"

"Yes, with Rajani in my arms I felt I was the luckiest person in the world. In a few months she found she was pregnant and like a true maverick she would point to her tummy and keep telling everyone, 'Look, look at my illegitimate child! I feel sooooo liberated!' I was scandalised, why was she calling it an illegitimate child? I told her, we should get married. She was mostly in a drunken stupor those days. She said she doesn't care, anyway, marriage was a bourgeois institution creating false bondage, but she agreed 'just out of fun'. So we got married and I entered the gates of hell with a smile on my leaps and fear of the unknown in my heart."

"Didn't you invite your parents?"

"Ha! That would have been so traditional, so conformist! Rajani would have none of that. So we got married first and went later to get their blessings. First we spent a few days with her parents. They were neither happy nor unhappy. They didn't care. Her father had got some posting abroad for three years and they were getting ready to leave. I took her to my parents; my mother shut the door on us, because Rajani looked so pregnant that my mother felt scandalised. We stayed in a hotel for two days and returned to Delhi. Our daughter was born three months after our wedding. Both of us got jobs as lecturers. As the daughter grew, we drifted apart. Rajani never forgave me for the way my parents had insulted her. Suddenly she found all the faults in the world in me. My parents were worse than tribals, they belonged to the jungle, someone like me who didn't know how to use a fork was not fit to live among civilised people, my English was worse than that of a village school master...........At one time she had loved me so intensely, now her dislike of me was equally intense. Once our daughter started going to school Rajani forbade her to speak to me, she told her if she picked up the funny accent from daddy, she would be good enough to become only a vegetable vendor selling vegetable from door to door. And one day she took our daughter to her parents in Trivandrum and left her with them. My world came crashing on me, my last hope of some semblance of a stable family life was lost forever. After that it was only a downhill journey for me, walking on a path strewn with red hot ember. You can never understand the pain, my friend, no one can."

"What happened to the girl?"

"Our daughter? She grew up to be a bigger nonconformist than her mother. In her late thirties now, she never married and is in a live-in relationship with a Chinese student in Singapore. Rajani runs away to be with them whenever she can."

"No, I was asking about the girl in the park, of forty one years ago."

"Oh, that girl? Honest to God, I don't know what happened to her. I had not written a single letter to her from JNU, her parents would have been livid if the letter fell into their hands. Moreover, I was so besotted with Rajani from the day I saw her. In the first summer vacation I went to Bhubaneswar,

I tried to hide from the girl down the street, by that time Rajani had moved into my room and we were living together......
.I don't know where the girl would be today, she may be in Bhubaneswar, in Indore or in Nagpur, but I know wherever she is she would be like the loveliest flower in a garden where there would be the fragrance of joy and the flavour of love. Whenever I see rains in the afternoon, I feel like running to a lawn and stand near a flower bed. How I wish, how achingly I wish, by some miracle, she would stand with me, and together we would look at the flowers. I would tell her - didn't you say I would forget you, like everyone does? Is there some way I can convince you, not only did I not forget you, hardly a day passes when I don't remember you! You are tucked away in a corner of my heart like one of these soft, smiling flowers, never to fade, never to wilt.........."

GLOSSARY

Dahlia – A beautiful winter flower

LSD – A psychedelic drug

JNU – Jawaharlal Nehru University

THE MAN IN RED SHIRT

Evening was creeping up like a silent shadow on an azure sky when Gautam got down from the train. The station was crowded. The train had disgorged hundreds of weary passengers. Rairangpur, a northern town of the state, was the final destination of the train. Gautam looked around. He needed no porter; he had only a small suitcase which he could carry by himself.

Suddenly, Gautam jerked himself to attention. A man in a red shirt, standing a few feet away, lost in the crowd, was looking intently at him. Gautam felt he had seen this man earlier, but could not remember where. He looked so familiar, like a part of his past. The smooth face, the sharp eyes, and that smile! The mocking smile, a challenge to Gautam, asking him to come near and get to know him better.

Unknown to him, Gautam felt drawn to the man and started walking towards him. He pushed the crowd around him to reach the man, but missed him. Somehow the man vanished in a flash. Gautam felt frustrated, he wished he could have met the man and asked him why he looked so familiar, why his face is hidden beneath a heap of memory, where had they met earlier, why the sharp eyes and the mocking smile were making him so unnerved, so drawn towards him.

Gautam started walking towards the exit. He again saw the glimpse of a red shirt, exactly similar to what the man was wearing. The man in the red shirt was getting out of the station. Gautam followed him, hoping to catch up with him. Outside the station there was chaos, a sort of mayhem. Taxiwallahs, auto rickshaw drivers and rickshaw pullers were competing with each other to entice passengers, shouting and trying to grab their luggage. Suddenly a fight broke out among them; a taxi driver was slapped by an auto wallah.

Gautam shuddered at the scene and steered clear of it. He came out of the auto stand and wondered whether to take a left or right turn in search of a hotel. He had come for a surprise visit, his first to this town, to investigate why the sale of the mosquito repellant Allout had suddenly dipped drastically. Someone had phoned him to inform that the retailers had been bribed by the Good Knight wholesaler. As the Regional Sales Manager of Johnson's he had been worried, he could not afford to lose customers of his product.

Gautam again had a flash of the red shirt on the road in the right. The man was so near! Walking fast, Gautam thought he could catch up with him. He was desperate, trying hard to remember where he had seen that face earlier. Was the man in the same school or college as him, though not in the same class? Was he in the neighbouring seat in a movie hall or a football stadium, absent mindedly picking up a few popcorns from Gautam's packet? Or was he a co-passenger in a train journey? Where had he seen those piercing eyes and the mysterious smile?

Gautam tried to take a swift look at his surroundings. This was his first trip to the small town, yet somehow he felt familiar here. It was like many other small towns he had visited, yet there was something special here. He felt something stirring inside him, a feeling of dejavu, a longing for some intimate memory. As if this town was a part of his destiny, he was bound to come here someday.

Gautam could see the red shirt off and on among the crowd walking ahead of him. He thought the man stopped at some point and looked back. A shiver ran down Gautam's spine. Somehow the sharp look and the cunning, challenging smile unnerved him further. He quickened his pace and came to the spot where the man had stopped. There was a sign on the left. Hotel Amar: AC Room 800 Non-AC 500. Gautam thought the rate was reasonable and he could stay there for the night. His return ticket was booked for the next evening. He looked ahead searching for the man in the red shirt, but he had vanished again. Gautam felt disappointed, would he see the man again? God knows! But somehow he wanted to meet him, even for once, just to ask him who he was and why he looked so familiar.

Gautam wanted to have an early dinner and go to sleep. Next day was going to be busy in meeting a few retailers and trying to get a feedback from the customers. He missed his wife, the children and was eager to return home. In his job he was used to frequent travelling and absence from home. But somehow this time he felt different. His twelve year old daughter Sangita had been upset with him this morning when he left. Dussehra was a few days away, she wanted to go to the market with him and buy a good 'modern' dress, not the type her Mom got her on birthdays and other festivals.

Satyakam, his son, was indifferent to dresses, his obsession was video games. He also wanted Gautam to take him to the market and buy a few video games for Dussehra. And Madhavi, his wife, she wanted nothing, except that Gautam should stay with the family all the time, and avoid so many tours.

He missed Madhavi like never before and dialed her number. She picked up on the first ring, as if she was waiting for this call.

"Reached? Why didn't you call earlier? I have been waiting!"

Gautam felt happy, to be wanted, to be missed.

"I tried a couple of times, but the connectivity from the train was poor."

"Good room? Do you have a tea maker in the room or you have to order room service for tea?"

Gautam smiled to himself, Madhavis's eyes for details!

"A fairly decent room. No tea maker! For eight hundred rupees a night you can't expect a tea maker in the room! What are the kids doing? Is Sangita still upset with me? Tell her I will take her out and buy the best available dress in the market this Sunday. Is she busy studying? Can you give the phone to her?"

Madhavi chuckled from the other side, "Studying? Are you dreaming? Your darling daughter is busy talking to her friend Suman, God knows what these silly girls talk about all the time. Just imagine she is not even a teen yet and so much to gossip! And when I go near her she makes a face and warns her friend on the other side that her Mom is close by, as if they are exchanging state secrets and presence of an intruder will compromise the country's security!"

Gautam tried to remind her that she was also a twelve year old once and must be talking to her friends for hours. Madhavi was horrified, "Me? Talking on the phone? Na Baba, Na, we didn't have mobile phones those days and the office phone sitting on a cradle like an old man draped in a black coat was too intimidating. And you know what your princess is busy doing these days?"

Gautam sat up, what is Sangita doing that Madhavi wants to report over the phone?

"What? Is she planning to blow up her school as a mark of protest against homework?"

Madhavi laughed, "No something more serious than that! She and her friends are exchanging jokes and pictures which are decidedly obscene."

"Oh my God! How do you know?"

"When she is in the bath room I regularly open up her message box to read the messages."

Gautam wanted to pull her leg,

"No, no, what I meant was how did you know the messages are obscene? You always claim you come from a very cultured family, which doesn't know anything obscene, doesn't use a bad word and if a carnal thought crosses someone's mind, he has to go and take a cold water bath!"

It was Madhavi's turn to feel playful, "Oh, that? Don't you know? All obscene things I learnt from you after marriage! I had come to you as a pure, virginal soul, O Krishna, my playful master; you corrupted my mind and filled me with a passion which you only could satisfy!"

Gautam felt an intoxicating thrill run through his veins at the seductive innuendo from his wife. He could not wait for the night to pass and he would board the train next evening to go home. They talked for some more time, Satyakam had already gone to sleep, he had a football match in the school and had returned home tired. Gautam ordered room service for dinner and went off to sleep.

The next morning Gautam started early. The town was small. Like many other towns the landscape was pleasantly familiar. A main street with shops lining on both sides, lanes and bylanes clogged with crowd and small stalls, street side vendors selling clothes, footwear and utensils, noise all around, bulls, dogs and buffaloes roaming around freely and small urchins begging - almost all Indian towns get their typical smell and flavour from the cauldron of human activity and penchant for gregariousness.

A small market building with elevated shops drew his attention and for a moment he stood still. He had a feeling that he was being watched and he had no doubt the man in the red shirt was somewhere nearby, with his piercing gaze and cunning smile. He looked around and spotted him. There, behind the footwear shop, partly hidden by plastic curtains providing shed to the shop! The man looked at Gautam, his smile became more pronounced as if he was trying to say something to him. Gautam felt uneasy, extremely nervous. Keeping the man steady in his sight he started walking towards him. The man was standing there unmoved, as if silently beckoning Gautam to come near.

Suddenly there was a rush, a group of families emerging out of the adjacent restaurant and for a few seconds Gautam lost sight of the man. Next moment the man was gone.

Disappeared, as if he was never there. Gautam wondered what happened to the man. He asked the footwear seller, but got nothing from him. Since the man in the red shirt was not a customer the shop keeper had not noticed him.

Gautam left the shop. His uneasy feeling had increased. He felt a mild drumming of the heart, the constant hide and seek game was eating into his consciousness like a nagging pain. He approached his first retailer and started discussing the strategy to increase the sale of Allout. But half his mind was busy wondering why the man in the red shirt was appearing and disappearing from Gautam's sight. He went to two more shops, his nervous feeling gradually giving way to his professional spirit. He assured an increased incentive to the retailers and they were happy.

It was getting close to lunch hour. Gautam decided to visit one more shop before getting back to the hotel for lunch. The fourth retailer was a serious sort of person and the discussion went on for some time. Gautam was getting hungry, his attention span was reducing and he was feeling a slight dizziness. Suddenly, the retailer before him started to dissolve from his sight and the man in the red shirt materialised from nowhere. The man was talking but his words became jumbled up and instead of hearing him, Gautam only saw a man with a smooth, oily face, a pair of glinting eyes and a very strange smile. For a few moments Gautam's mind went blank, hearing nothing, feeling nothing. He returned to his sense when the retailer started shouting at him.

The retailer was worried, he gave a glass of Limca to Gautam and dropped him back at the hotel in his motor cycle. Gautam straight went to the dining hall to order lunch. A short, burly man in suit and tie was waiting for his lunch.

Gautam badly craved for some company, to talk to someone and unburden himself. He asked the man if he could sit on the chair opposite. The man seemed happy to have someone to talk to.

"New to this town? Is this your first visit?"

"Yes, just for a day. Returning home by the night train."

"Ah, how can you leave so early? It's such a beautiful place, surrounded by small, green hills. There is a huge waterfall about five kilometres away. And the forests, the deep forests full of birds and animals about ten kilometres from here! You must visit them, if not this time, during your next visit. Where do you come from? What's your name?"

"I am Gautam Tripathy, from Bhubaneswar. And you?"

"I am Godabarish Mishra, Professor of Philosophy at the Sambalpur University. I come to this town often to deliver lectures. I have a sizeable fan following here. If you were staying tonight I would have invited you to attend my lecture in the Town Hall in the evening"

"So sorry. My train leaves at seven in the evening. What is the lecture about?"

The professor chuckled,

"'India's Hour of Birth and Her Destiny'. I am a deep believer in Astrology"

Gautam was amused,

"Does the country have a destiny? That too governed by an hour of birth?"

The professor became serious. Their food had arrived. A huge, cooked, head of a fish was staring at Gautam from the Professor's plate. Gautam had ordered a vegetarian lunch. The professor attacked the head of the fish with great gusto, he was happy to get a captive audience, "Every living being has a destiny, pre-ordained from the moment of his birth".

Gautam tried to pull the professor's leg, "Even this fish? Was it born to die for you?"

"Yes, just imagine, this fish must have been caught from the river which passes through this town, if the fish had managed to swim a kilometre further, it might have escaped getting caught and might have lived for one more year. Or it would have been caught by someone else and would not have come to this hotel. And if some other person had taken lunch before me and ordered head of fish it would have landed up in his plate. But this fish was destined to be consumed by me."

"But it sounds so frivolous! A fish and its destiny!"

"Nothing is frivolous my friend in this world, particularly for every being which breathes to live. Every breath is a footfall of its destiny. And the country is a leaving being, breathing through her one billion people. You must have read about Delhi's Khan Market incident last week. The poor fellow had come to buy chicken tikka for his wife and got into a brawl with a brat over a parking spot. They had a big argument and the brat stabbed the poor chap to death. Can you see the connection with destiny? The dead man used to live in Vasant Kunj, a good ten kilometres away, he could have gone to at least half a dozen other places, to Rajinder Dhaba near Kamal Cinema, to Kakeda's in Connaught Place, Karim's in Nizamuddin, or Colonel's Kebab in Defence Colony. He could have got chicken tikka for his wife in the evening or even one hour earlier or later, but destiny brought him to Khan Market at that hour, to a particular spot, precisely when the killer brat was parking his car. My present research is about the stellar constellation at the midnight hour of 15th August 1947 and to decipher our country's destiny. I have found some interesting facts and will share them with the audience tonight. I firmly believe everyone's destiny is contained in a package of data. This data is maintained by God and very few highly enlightened astrologers have the ability to access a fraction of that data."

Gautam was astounded,

"You mean God maintains data for more than six billion people spread over the world?"

Professor Mishra flashed a benign smile, "Are you doubting the infinite power of God? Is there a limit to what He can do? Even your coming to this town is a part of your destiny, our meeting here today at this moment in this dining hall is preordained, everything is predestined my friend, I can give you a few more instances….."

Suddenly a waiter appeared at the side of Prof. Mishra and handed him a piece of paper. The Professor had finished his meal, he got up and smiled at Gautam, "Sorry young man, I have to leave, some people are waiting in the lobby, I had promised them I would visit the Philosophy Department of the local college at two thirty. Hope we will meet again, if you happen to come to Sambalpur, please look me up at the University. I will be happy to share many interesting stories with you".

Gautam left the hotel at three, he wanted to visit four more retailers before returning to the hotel and leaving for the railway station to catch the train. The thought of the man in the red shirt returned to his mind. Would he appear again, at some unexpected turn, in some narrow lane or behind some lonely shop? Luckily, Gautam didn't see him during his visit to the four retailers.

Around six he started walking back to the hotel. Lights were yet to come up in the town. It was still bright, the air was stuffy, hot and humid, probably it would get cool later in the evening. Lots of people had come out to the market with their families for shopping. Dussehra was round the corner and the festive season had already arrived with promises of fun and celebrations. Gautam's attention was drawn to a young couple walking ahead of him, the father holding the hand of their small child. The boy must be around four years old. He was pointing at some toys hanging from a string in a shop.

The parents had moved near the shop to look at the toys more closely. The father's grip must have loosened a bit. The small boy drifted away and started walking towards the middle of the road. Gautam was hardly a foot away, his heart almost stopped at the sight of the speeding Innova car coming from the opposite direction. In a couple of moments it would run over the boy! With a cry Gautam lunged forward and brought the child back to the side of the road, but lost control of himself. Next moment the Innova hit him hard and threw him high up in the air. Before Gautam's head hit the road he looked at the car helplessly. There, sitting on the bonnet of the Innova was the man in the red shirt, his face solemn, as if he was carrying out a preordained, pre-assigned job against his wish. His cunning smile was gone, but the eyes had not lost any of their penetrative intensity. There was a strange melancholy on his face.

In his dying moments, Gautam felt an incredible sadness, for leaving his dear Madhavi, his darling Sangita and the precious Satyakam. His eyes met the eyes of the man in the red shirt and he whispered, "So you are Death and you have been stalking me, perhaps ever since I was born! That's why you looked so much a part of my past! I wish I had known you yesterday. Had I recognised you for what you are, I wouldn't have followed you to the hotel and returned to my dear family last evening itself! Now you are taking me away, who will look after them? They will miss me, who will buy dress for my Sangita and video games for my Satyakam? Who will talk to my Madhavi, promising her all the love in the world? Who will………..As life ended for him, Gautam's words remained suspended in a cruel, oppressive evening air in a small, crowded town, the last town he would ever visit.

GLOSSARY

Dussehra – The famous festival of Odisha and Bengal, celebrating the slaying of the Demon Mahisasura by Goddess Durga

– 11 –

UNRESOLVED

I looked at Simadri. His eyes were closed, head bent, as if he was in deep sleep. Yet, in the terribly shaking train, I knew he must be awake, as awake as a brooding rabbit. Coromandel Express was speeding away like a train possessed. I suspected, Simadri somehow was not concerned. I was not sure if he even wanted it to reach a destination. Ever since we boarded the train at Vijaywada in the late afternoon, Simadri had not uttered a single word, kept his eyes closed, pretending to sleep. I was eager to talk to him, to know what exactly had happened, how he landed up in a jail. Yes, a jail, of all the places! Our quiet, dignified friend, rounded up by the police in a midnight raid at Swapna Lodge in Vijaywada, picked up, along with eleven others, for "immoral" activities. I still believed there was some terrible mix-up and Simadri, my college mate would come out of it with no scratches.

"Here, Simadri, have some tea, it's piping hot and very sweet, exactly the way you like it."

He shook his head, confirming my suspicion that behind the closed eyes, the mind was quite alert. I persisted,

"I have ordered rice and chicken curry, your favourite food for dinner, we will get it at Vijaynagaram, one hour from now. You must be hungry, did you eat anything in the morning?"

Simadri kept mum. Frankly, I was running out of patience. Why was this idiot behaving as if he had been wronged by others? It was I who had paid for his bail after the lawyer I engaged appeared before the magistrate and got his bail approved. So who was he trying to fool? A slow, smouldering anger was rising in me. I kept it under control.

In fact, I had undergone a terrible mix of emotions since yesterday morning, from the moment I opened the morning newspaper and stumbled into a small piece of news in some innocuous corner under the heading, "Odia man taken to custody in Vijaywada." I was curious to know why a man from Odisha would be a guest of the jail authorities in Vijaywada. The next moment I shrieked, as if struck by lightning. Simadri Nayak? Our Simadri? In jail? I had no doubt it was my college mate Simadri, because the name itself was sort of unique, something like Michael Mishra or Kamruddin Panigrahi! I also knew Simadri, as a pharmaceutical agent, used to go to Vijaywada to get his bulk stock of medicines. So, the scoundrel was also eating the forbidden fruit in the lodges of Vijaywada, away from home! Such a Chhupa Rustam!

I remembered I had his wife Vijaya's number somewhere in the telephone book. I quickly found it and called. The phone was switched off. I called again, maybe there was some mistake, but again I got the message that the phone was switched off. In a flash of rare brilliance, it occurred to me that I should contact Simadri to confirm if it was indeed he who was warming a bed in some forlorn cell of a Vijaywada jail. The fact that the message of "switched off" came in Telugu convinced me that Simadri was in an alien land, away from friends and family. I thought of waking up my wife Kalyani to break this sensational news to her, but I thought it would be prudent to go to Simadri's house first, hoping against hope that the news was wrong and Simadri was enjoying a sound sleep at home in pure domestic bliss.

The house was locked. There was no one nearby, as if the news of Simadri in jail had spread like wild fire and everyone in the neighbourhood was keeping indoors to disown any familiarity with the immoral leper. That stopped me from asking anyone where Vijaya would have gone with her daughter Gayatri. With a heavy heart and restless mind I spent a few hours in my office and boarded the train to Vijaywada in the afternoon. I knew Simadri needed someone to rescue him from the clutches of law and that someone was destined to be me. From the newspaper I had gathered a brief idea of his brush with law. It seemed the police had conducted a midnight raid on the Swapna Lodge on a tipoff and found sixteen couples in "flagrante delicto", while engaged in immoral activities. They could arrest only twelve culprits, the others managed to flee under the cover of darkness. Our friend Simadri was one of the "dirty dozen".

It was past midnight when I checked into a hotel near Vijaywada railway station. In the morning I rushed to Swapna Lodge. The manager, who himself had managed to get a bail the previous evening was suitably embarrassed to meet a friend of one of the victims. He helped me to contact his lawyer, who seemed to be an old hand at getting bail for deserving delinquents in exchange of an appropriate fee. Simadri was granted bail a little after one o clock and we boarded the Coromandal Express at three. Simadri had not spoken a word to me from the moment I met him outside the jail - not even a word of thanks. He was lost in his own world, pretending to go off to sleep when we found our berths.

The dinner was served at nine. Simadri said he was not hungry and I blew a fuse,

"Hey idiot, what do you mean, not hungry? You think you are a bloody superman who will survive a night without food? If you are such a superman how did you get caught? In an act of sin?"

Simadri sat up, like he had been stung by a bee,

"Sin? What sin? I committed no sin. I was a freaking guest at the Lodge."

I refused to believe him. From the lawyer I had read the charge sheet filed by the police. My anger was threatening to go out of control,

"Just a guest? Then who was the woman who ran away from your room at the sight of the police? Since when have you started sleeping with sluts?"

Simadri collapsed as if I had hit him with a huge slap. I will never forget the sadness that spread over his face, like a dark cloud over a clear sky. He held his face with both hands and mumbled feebly,

"Padmaja! Her name is Padmaja and she is not a slut! Please don't insult her."

Simadri got up and ran out of the cubicle. I found him a few minutes later standing near the door of the compartment and smoking a cigarette. My anger had subsided at his outburst – to know that there was another woman in Simadri's life, a stranger to us, who he respected enough to defend.

I went to him and gently tapped him on the shoulder. The hurt in his eyes was palpable, I knew soon he would tell me his story. I didn't want to hurry him,

"Come, let's eat. I can foresee the long battle you have ahead of you. At least eat and fortify yourself for the morning. God knows when you will get another meal of rice and chicken curry again."

Simadri picked at his food, his mind obviously elsewhere. The dinner over, we sat smoking. I looked at him,

"Simadri, will you tell me what has happened to you? Why did you need a Padmaja to come to your life, when you have Vijaya and Gayatri at home?"

Simadri flinched, as if I had pricked him with a sharp needle,

"Home? It's no freaking home Abhijeet, it's a hell for me. For the last two years I have been living like a stranger in that dungeon, bound by four stinking walls."

"What? Frankly, it's a shock to hear this. You and Vijaya look like a perfectly happy couple to everyone. Why do you say home is a hell for you?"

Simadri flashed a pathetic smile,

"It's all a facade, a charade played by Vijaya to make it appear she is such a sweet, nice wife! Didn't someone say everyone is like a moon and has a dark side which he doesn't show to others?"

"What dark side? Don't talk in riddles! Please!"

"Nirmal, when you return home in the evening what does Kalyani do?"

"Do? What do you mean do? She would have made tea and would be waiting for me, we would have tea and snacks together, she would pour out all the stories of the day to me, we would talk to the kids before sending them to do their homework. I presume that's how it must be in everyone's house. It's just routine."

Simadri surprised me by breaking into a sob,

"It's just routine....it's just routine. No, my friend, it's not routine, not in my home. Vijaya just waits like a crouching animal, to pounce on me and shred me to pieces the moment I enter home. If I return early she would say should I not work harder to earn more money, do I realize my income is less than that of a peon in a government office? If I return late, she would fire a different salvo, am I aware of my responsibilities towards the family, should I stay out of home all the time? If I try to play with my daughter, she would come screaming, do I have any business to spoil her studies, do I want Gayatri to turn out to be an useless good-for-nothing person like her father? And if I don't play with her, she would blame me – do I want our only daughter to become a psycho, a mental wreck, neglected by the father, deprived of paternal love? If I buy a gift for her and for Gayatri, she would accuse me of throwing away money as if I was a king's illegitimate offspring, if I don't buy a gift when I return from tour she would throw tantrums like I am a beggar returning home with an empty begging bowl. Sometimes I would be so scared of her shouting that I would feel like not ringing the door bell, preferring to sleep in the verandah outside. So many times I have thought of not returning to the hell called home, I have felt like jumping before a train and end everything. I know it wouldn't make any difference to her. She has written me off as a husband, or even as a person. It is so exasperating that for the last two years I have almost stopped talking to her. We are living under the same roof, but as strangers."

I was stunned hearing this. We had met Simadri and his wife a couple of times in the past two years, but had no inkling of such a storm in their life.

"What about your daughter Gayatri? She doesn't talk to you?"

Simadri sighed,

"Only the minimum. You see, I stay out of home on tour for at least fifteen days a month. God knows what poison Vijaya fills in our daughter's ears. She avoids talking to me, except when she needs anything. How I wish the three of us would sit, chat, have our meals together. But Vijaya makes it impossible, shouting at me all the time, belittling me, humiliating me and making my life worse than hell."

My friend kept quiet, looking down in despair. I wondered when he went into the orbit of the other woman, his Padmaja,

"And Padmaja, when did you meet her?"

Simadri looked up, the memory of the woman who he obviously loved, brought a smile to his face.

"Ah, Padmaja! She is exactly what Vijaya is not - sweet, compassionate and understanding, the time I spend with her are the best moments I can dream of, a solace in the dreary desert of my life."

"Is she beautiful? An apsara?"

Simadri smiled again, it was nice to see him smile after a long day of desperate aloofness.

"No, she is anything but an apsara. She is of course tall, slim, of wheatish complexion. Her face is captivating, the eyes expressive. The first time I saw her, my heart melted, looking at her sad, deep eyes. She had lost her husband a year before and left with a seven years old daughter to look after, she had returned to her parent's home. She started working as an accountant at the medicine wholesaler's firm. I went to her to check the bills and just sat there looking at her without blinking my eyes. I felt as if I was a weary traveller wandering aimlessly and at last found the path of peace and love. Every time she looked at me my heart did a somersault. I went again next day, bought some more medicines and sat at her table, just inhaling the fragrance of her presence. She must have sensed it, but said nothing. Her gentle talk, sweet manner won me over, making me fall like a ton of bricks on a pile of sand. I went back to Vijaywada after a week and thereafter every week. At home I didn't care what Vijaya told me, because I was like a man possessed, only thinking of my next visit to Vijaywada when I would meet the sweet and gentle Padmaja. A month after we met, she told her parents that she had to go on tour and we spent two nights in a lodge, registering as husband and wife. Believe me Nirmal, those were the best forty eight hours of my life. I could never imagine, love between two gentle souls could make life so blissful."

Simadri stopped and closed his eyes, perhaps reliving those happy moments. His face had got back some glow and I was surprised that despite the prospect of the impending disaster of next morning he could feel so much at peace with himself.

I was curious to know what happened to Padmaja when Simadri got arrested. I asked him. He flashed a sly smile,

"After talking to her, the police knew she was not a call girl, still they demanded twenty thousand rupees to let her go. I paid it promptly. For me they put the price at fifty thousand.

I didn't have it. Padmaja promised to borrow the amount and come back as soon as she could. She fell at the feet of the policemen and pleaded not to arrest me. I forbade her not to get involved, I didn't want anyone to point a finger at her. She left for home crying."

"So, Mr. Romeo, what is your plan now? I am sure you are not exactly looking forward to meeting Vijaya in the morning!"

Simadri closed his eyes and pretended to go to sleep.

After we got down from the train at Bhubaneswar in the early hours of next morning, we went to Simadri's house. It was locked. Simadri knew Vijaya must have left for her cousin Priya's place and wanted to go there immediately. I asked him to calm down and brought him to my home. After a quick bath and breakfast we went to Priya's house in my motorbike.

We rang the bell and after a long wait Priya opened the door. She didn't invite us to come in, probably her husband was not at home. For about five minutes we heard she and Vijaya talking loudly, arguing things out. Then she came to the door and told Simadri to wait. Only I was asked to get in. Vijaya was standing in the open courtyard, I went near her, slowly, like someone accused of a serious felony, appearing before a judge. She just stood there, looking at me, her eyes red with anger. I quietly murmured,

"I had gone to your house day before yesterday in the morning. It was locked."

She shouted back, "Yes, what do you expect me to do? Throw the doors open to allow friends and neighbours to come in and congratulate me, because my husband had become famous all over the country?"

With my head bent, I whispered,

"Simadri is truly repentant; will you please talk to him?"

She sprang up like a cobra uncoiled, her face distorted with vicious anger,

"Repentant! Aren't you ashamed to come before me to plead his case? Do you have any decency left? Just go and ask your friend if I had done something like this, shared a bed with some other person, would he have forgiven me? Go. Go and ask him and come back to me with an answer", she almost spat those words at me.

I made a last ditch effort,

"At least think of Gayatri. She needs a father's presence at home."

This time the cobra in Vijaya almost stung me, making me take a step back,

"Gayatri? What has he got to do with Gayatri? In fact my daughter will be better off without a shameless, characterless father like your friend. Here, take this key to the house. Give it to him and ask him to clear off with his things by the evening. That house has no place for him to spend a night. I am sure he will relish being at Gulab street, the red light area, finding his soul mate among the sluts. Now please leave, your presence reminds me of the shameful shadow lurking outside the door."

I knew I had lost the case, there was no way she would relent, even to meet Simadri. I turned to leave. She stopped me on the track, to deal another blow.

"Yes, tell your friend to send twenty thousand rupees every month for the next three months. By that time I will find a job to support myself and my daughter. I don't want to touch any money from him after that. But also tell him, if he thinks he can get rid of us and start a new family, he is sadly mistaken. I will never agree to a divorce. He deserves to roll on the muddy soil of the Gulab Streets and die a stinking death there. Now just get out. Leave us in peace."

I came out. Simadri had started walking down the street. No doubt, he had heard everything through the open door. His head was bent with worry, a grim grief had cast a shadow on his face. I started the motorbike and offered him a ride. He looked at me with unseeing eyes and waved me on, determined to walk the unresolved path of life with a quiet resignation.

GLOSSARY

Apsara – Beautiful as a fairy

Chhupa Rustam – A Romeo

Gulab Street – The red light area of the town

12

HYENA

The voice at the other end was fluctuating, but there was no mistaking who was on the line. Mantriji! After so many years! Amaresh was thrilled!

"Hello.o.o, Hello.o.o.o, is it Amaresh? Pehchaanaa? Are you able to place me?"

Place him? Of course he would place Mantriji from anywhere in the world! For five long years Amaresh had been like a shadow to him, officially he was Mantriji's PS, but he, Jyotsna and their two kids had almost become a part of his family. Amaresh replied to him, happiness brimming over his voice,

"Yes Sir, can I ever forget you, your affection for me and my family? I am just like a younger brother to you. Remember how often you used to say that? It's such a pleasant surprise to hear your voice after so many years!"

Mantriji was pleased,

"Yes, yes, theek hai, theek hai. I got your number from your old PA in the Ministry. How are you in your new place? Darangbadi?"

Amaresh wanted to correct Mantriji, the place was called Daringibadi, the only hill station in Odisha, a hundred and twenty kilometres away from Berhampur, the nearest big town. And it was no longer a new place for Amaresh, he and his family had shifted there eight years back, immediately after Amaresh quit his government job and decided to take up horticulture farming in this quaint little place, famous for its salubrious climate and fertile soil. After serving Mantriji as PS for five years, he had to return to the Ministry of Finance to report to his parent department, but somehow he was made to feel unwelcome. He was posted in a ministry where his boss was known to be difficult, throwing tantrums at the drop of a hat, shouting at subordinates and often flinging files at their face like guided missiles.

One evening after a particularly disgusting day he came home with a massive headache and asked Jyotsna whether she would like to quit Delhi forever. She was more than happy. A school teacher's daughter from the small town of Balasore she had never been able to adjust to the fast life of Delhi. So Amaresh resigned from service, spent a couple of weeks at Daringibadi to locate a chunk of twenty acres of land where he could raise his farm and live happily. The local school for the children was half a kilometre away, the air was pure, the water crystal clear and the surrounding forests, and hills with cascading streams made the kids feel at home and the parents happy beyond their wildest imagination.

Amaresh had lost touch with Rajesh Singh, his old boss, the Minister. The year Amaresh had got back to the Ministry, the minister lost the elections to the Lok Sabha. He went back to Chhatisgarh and next year became an MLA and a Minister in that state. After five years he again lost in the elections and his party also got unseated from power. The last he heard about Rajesh Singh, he had settled in Bilaspur, was active in politics and managing his three hotels and half a dozen petrol bunks.

Amaresh wondered how Rajesh Singh remembered him after so many years. As if Mantriji could read his mind, he spoke to Amaresh,

"I want to ask you a favour Amaresh, a very small one. I am sure you won't disappoint me".

"Please don't embarrass me saying that. Just tell me what you want. Your wish is my command".

Mantriji chuckled on the other side,

"I know, I know, I can always depend on you. Do you remember my son Ajay?"

"Yes, of course. He was such an active, vibrant boy those days. He must be around twenty years now?"

"Twenty two to be exact. After I returned to Chhatisgarh and became a minister here, he became extra active, bunking school, enjoying life and spending money like a Maharaja. Got into some wrong company and picked up some bad habits. I want him to spend a couple of months with you and your family so that he can become a good man again. I want you to exert some positive influence on him and teach him the good ways of life".

"Yes sir, I will do my best. When is he coming?"

Mantriji laughed, an open hearted, cunning laugh,

"He has already left for Darangbadi, with an attendant. His train should reach Berhampur by ten in the morning, he should reach your place by two o clock."

Amaresh was startled. How come Mantriji did not think of asking him first before sending Ajay to live with his family? Mantriji had anticipated this doubt,

"Actually he had to leave in a hurry. Some of my political opponents are targeting him to settle score with me. Amaresh, please take good care of him. And make sure nobody knows he is with you. This is absolutely important. If my opponents come to know he is in Darangbadi, they will come after him. There could be fireworks because of that. Politicians and their followers are not very civilised in this part of the country."

Before Amaresh could ask any more questions the phone got disconnected. He wanted to call back, to ask a few questions, did the Mantriji mean that Ajay was to be kept in hiding, not stepping out of the house at all? What did he mean by fireworks? But Rajesh Singh had called from an unlisted number; there was no way Amaresh could call him back.

Next afternoon around two thirty a tall, handsome young man alighted from a taxi, accompanied by a short, dark person who carried his master's stroller bag into the house. Ajay bent and touched the feet of Amaresh and Jyotsna. They were happy to see this nice, well mannered, soft spoken young man who was more like a grown up boy. They all had lunch together and Ajay's attendant left after two hours. He had to catch the night train back to Bilaspur.

When the kids came back from school, they were really happy to meet the big Bhaiya. They were thrilled that they could speak to him in Hindi - their Hindi had got rusted after they left Delhi. The expensive chocolates brought from Bilaspur were grabbed by them and finished in no time. Fifteen years old Kamalesh and Kajal, younger to him by a year and half, soon became great fans of Ajay Bhaiya. There was a door from Ajay's room opening outside to the farm, Ajay set up a badminton court there and they played in the evenings after school.

At the dining table Ajay showed impeccable manners addressing Amaresh as uncle and Jyotsna as Aunty. He would help Jyotsna carry the plates to the kitchen, despite her forbidding him to do so. Amaresh and Jyotsna's room was next to Ajay's. After a few days of Ajay's stay, Jyotsna heard a slight creak in the door one night after everyone had gone to sleep. She went to the window and peeped out. In the dark a light was glowing, it was clear someone was smoking a cigarette. She got terribly scared. What was this boy doing, didn't he know, it was an open farm and all kinds of animals came there in the night?

The next morning at the breakfast table Amaresh suggested to Ajay that he should not go out into the open in the night. Ajay smiled,

"What will happen if I go out?"

"Animals often come into the farm looking for a stray hen or a rabbit."

Ajay's tone got slightly harsh, surprising Amaresh and Jyotsna,

"What kinds of animals?"

"Jackals, foxes and sometimes hyenas, all violent and dangerous species."

Ajay dismissed them with a derisive laugh,

"You think I am scared of them? I am a Rajput, I can kill them with my bare hands."

Amaresh and Jyotsna looked at each other; this was a different Ajay, over-confident, arrogant and reckless! They had not seen him like this before. The next moment Ajay softened,

"Uncle, please don't worry, I won't step out in the night unless it is absolutely necessary".

Jyotsna checked for the next two nights. Ajay didn't go out.

The attendant Preetam came exactly on the fifteenth day. Ajay was waiting eagerly for him. Preetam left after two hours. That evening Ajay was restless before dinner. In the night the glow of cigarettes reappeared in the open. It also lasted a long time.

In a few days balmy October nights gave way to chilly November weather. Winter was known to be quite severe in Daringibadi, occasionally going below zero degree temperature. Ajay had been in the Amaresh home for almost three weeks. Outwardly calm, it was obvious he was getting restless. One evening Kamalesh came running to Jyotsna,

"Mummy, you know what, Ajay Bhaiya has a pistol, he showed it to me today. You know, he said he has shot three people with that pistol. He showed me how to shoot and we killed a rabbit in the dense part of the farm."

Jyotsna was horrified! Teaching shooting to a fifteen year boy! Had Ajay gone out of his mind? At the dinner Amaresh asked him if it was true that he had killed three persons with his pistol. Ajay smiled,

"No uncle, I was just bragging, just wanted to impress Kamalesh."

"Please don't show that pistol to him again and for heaven's sake don't teach him shooting, understand?"

"Yes uncle", Ajay was his usual humble, well-mannered self.

Two days later early at dawn, Jyotsna got up suddenly to the sound of clothes being washed, the unmistakable sound of soap being rubbed against dresses startled her. Who was washing clothes? So early in the cold morning!

She came out. To her horror she found Ajay washing everyone's clothes, dipping them in water, rubbing them with soap and rinsing them. The bundle had her clothes and Kajal's also! What a shame, how scandalous! Ajay's face was flushed, his eyes were red, it appeared he had not slept in the night. She shouted at him,

"What are you doing, why are you washing our clothes? Who told you to touch my garments? Get up, go to your room."

Ajay looked at her and smiled,

"Aunty, am I not a part of your family now? Please let me help."

Amaresh had got up at the noise and come out. He was amused to see Ajay sitting cross legged like a yogi and washing clothes with full dedication!

Jyotsna was still shouting at Ajay,

"Ajay, get up immediately and go back to your room!"

Ajay smiled again and took out a blouse of Jyotsna's and a dress of Kajal's, he started rubbing the soap on them. That's when it struck Amaresh how wrong it was. He thundered at Ajay to stop what he was doing and go to his room. Ajay looked sheepishly at them and walked to his room slowly. Jyotsna remained worried throughout the day. What was this young man up to?

That night the humming started in Ajay's room. It was clear Ajay was humming a song alternating between a high pitch and a low pitch, he would come near the connecting door to Amaresh and Jyotsna's room and start whispering a song in a very low voice. Amaresh was a deep sleeper, but Jyotsna slept light. She got up, she could feel Ajay standing near the door, almost leaning on it. His breath was heavy, the whisper was persistent, the song indistinct. She shook Amaresh to wake him up, the sound on the other side stopped. Annoyed, Amaresh went back to sleep. And the humming started again, rising to a soft crescendo and petering off to a slow whisper. Jyotsna had a restless night.

Next morning everything was normal. Ajay was on his best behaviour, head bent, munching his breakfast slowly and talking politely to Amaresh and Jyotsna. But from then on night was a different story, Ajay's humming started the moment Amaresh went off to sleep. It was a peculiar sound, starting as a whisper like a snake hissing and turning into a slow hum like a bee humming. It got on Jyotsna's nerves. And the worst was when she could see the shadow of Ajay's feet under the door as if he was leaning on the door and panting slowly, rhythmically. What was he doing, and why? How long would he stay at Daringibadi? An unknown fear had gripped Jyotsna, as if the young man staying with them was highly abnormal, during the day he was good manners personified, but with the night deepening, he turned into some kind of a psycho, a monster with a turmoiled mind.

A few nights after that, the humming was accompanied by another frightening sound, the cry of a jackal, alternating with the howl of a dog, or the meow of cats. The sound was very subdued, as if Ajay was trying to make it appear like it was coming from somewhere in the farm. But Jyotsna had no doubt in her mind it was he who was producing those sounds. And the day a hyena entered into the farm, trying to break into the poultry shed, Ajay produced the sound of a hyena barking! Jyotsna woke up Amaresh and the moment Amaresh asked what was the matter, all sounds ceased in the adjoining room.

The next day Kajal came to Jyotsna, a heavy frown crowding her face,

"Mummy, how long Ajay Bhaiya is going to stay here? Why doesn't he go back to Bilaspur?"

Jyotsna looked up at her daughter, worried.

"Why? What happened? Why are you asking this question?"

"Mummy, somehow I don't feel comfortable in his presence any more. He looks at me in a very different way, which I don't like"

"What different way? Tell me clearly Kajal, be frank with me"

"Mummy, if someone talks to me, he will look at my face, right? Ajay Bhaiya's eyes keep roaming over my body, often staying fixed on my chest. I feel very uneasy when he does that. It's a creepy feeling. And sometimes he comes very close to me, trying to touch me, on my hand, my waist or my face, whispering that I am his darling sister."

Jyotsna felt the earth slipping from under her feet. She knew exactly what kind of perversion had gripped Ajay's mind!

"Beti, don't wear frocks at home any more, wear Salwar Kameez, cover your front with a dupatta all the time, please. Please be careful. I will speak to your daddy tonight; let him check with Mantriji how long he is planning to keep his son here."

Kajal was not happy about the restrictions in dress,

"Yes Mummy, please ask daddy to do that. But tell me, this is our house; why should we have to guard ourselves against an outsider? It's really getting very frustrating."

That evening after dinner Jyotsna posed the question to Amaresh, he also had no answer.

"I am not able to talk to Mantriji, he had called from an unlisted number, Ajay gave me a number of his father, but that phone is always switched off. I don't know how long he is going to hide his son here."

Jyotsna sat up,

"Hiding? Yes, I wonder why he is hiding his son here! What is Ajay hiding from? What has he done?"

Suddenly Amaresh remembered something,

"When is the next visit of Preetam? It must be somewhere close, he comes every fifteen days, right?"

"Yes, he comes on alternate Sundays. His next visit is due four days from now."

"This time I will go to Berhampur to pick him up. Let me try to get some idea about what Ajay is hiding from."

Next Sunday when Preetam got down from the train around ten in the morning, he was pleasantly surprised to see Amaresh waiting for him.

"Sahab aap? Yahan kaise?"

"I had come yesterday to buy some plants, pesticides and fertilisers. Since I was going back today I thought I would pick you up. It will save you the taxi fare."

"Yes Saab, very thoughtful of you, now I realise why Mantriji is so fond of you! Let me go and take a shower in the lodge and we will leave after an early lunch."

"Sure, some lunch and a couple of beer, may be!"

Preetam's eyes shone with anticipation,

"No Saab, no beer! Wine and Beer are for aristocrats like you, I will have whiskey, Royal Challenge is my favourite brand".

Amaresh looked at his watch.

"Sure, let's go".

By the time they reached Daringibadi after a sumptuous lunch, it was three in the afternoon. Jyotsna was waiting eagerly for Amaresh,

"Any news? Did Preetam say when will Ajay leave?"

Amaresh shook his head,

"Not in the near future, we are badly stuck with this monster. May be for two-three months."

Jyotsna cried out,

"Monster! What do you mean monster?"

"Not now, Ajay might hear us. I will tell you in the night."

"Do you know what he did last night; I almost fainted out of fear."

Amaresh sat up, waiting eagerly for Jyotsna to continue,

"We were watching a movie on TV after dinner. Ajay sat near Kajal. When everyone was immersed in the movie, unknown to me he slowly let his hand roam over Kajal's back. She wanted to get away from there but somehow he managed to pull her back. After about ten minutes he took his hand near her thighs and started squeezing them. I saw Kajal squirming and Ajay's hands on her thighs. I got the shock of my life. I didn't want to create a scene, since you were not at home. I simply switched off the TV and asked everyone to go to their rooms and sleep. In the night Ajay kept on humming and imitating the sound of animals. In the morning he wanted to take both the kids into the dense part of the farm to look for rabbits, I forbade them to go out. He has been sulking ever since. Now that he saw Preetam and the bag he is carrying, it cheers him up. I wonder what is it that Preetam brings with him which immediately uplifts Ajay's mood".

Amaresh shuddered,

"I know, I will tell you everything in the night."

Preetam left after two hours. Dinner was taken early. Jyotsna was impatient to hear what Ajay was up to.

Amaresh was deep in thought, curled on the bed, waiting for Jyotsna to come.

"You know, the person staying under the same roof with us for the last six weeks is a rapist, a murderer, and a drug addict…"

Before he could proceed further Jyotsna shrieked,

"What, do you realise what you are saying?"

Amaresh nodded, a deep worry crowding his face like dark clouds on a clear sky,

"Yes, after five pegs of whiskey, Preetam Singh opened up and sang like a parrot. Ajay is hiding because he had shot a man on the day he left for here; he was put on the train by Rajesh Singh before police could arrest him. He had committed two murders earlier but his father was a minister at the time and could suppress the cases. This time it was difficult because his party is not in power. A year back Ajay had also raped a young receptionist in one of their hotels, that case was also buried under the files. Preetam brings him charas and cocaine every fortnight. Ajay also injects himself with some drugs."

Jyotsna's face had collapsed like a paper bag,

"And the humming, the sound of animals?"

"It is a habit from Ajay's childhood. It seems he used to imitate all kinds of sounds perfectly and even now enjoys doing that. He also has a split personality, with elders he can be very polite and well-mannered. With others he can be extremely abrasive and arrogant."

Jyotsna started crying, tears flowing from her eyes copiously,

"O My God, what kind of mess your Mantriji has pushed us in? Of all the people in the world he chose you to be saddled with this monster! Is this the price you pay for being decent, polite and helpful to people? What to do now? Tomorrow morning you tell Ajay to leave, we can send one of our farm boys to accompany him to Bilaspur."

"No. No, let's not commit that mistake. Preetam says Ajay has a mercurial temper and can become very violent if provoked, that's how he committed those murders. We must think of our safety and that of the children. I was told by Preetam that Mantriji is trying his best to get the case withdrawn, but it may take two three months, or if the heavy amount of bribe works, it may happen earlier. Nobody knows for certain. Ajay has become very restless here; he is missing his girlfriend who is in Bilaspur. He is also putting pressure on his father to do something. Let's just wait for a few more days."

Amaresh went off to sleep. Jyotsna's mind was in deep turmoil. She heard the faintest sound of a door being opened. She peeped through the window, Ajay was walking like a shadow down the path to the huge sal tree where he would sit and smoke his charas. Jyotsna shuddered, remembering the way his hand had crept to Kajal's thighs. Was he already under the influence of some drugs at that time? Otherwise how could he do such a vile thing in the presence of Jyotsna?

The next morning Ajay was excessively polite to Jyotsna offering help in the kitchen. He was also eyeing Elizabeth, the young tribal maid who was bending over the wooden board cutting vegetables. His eyes were red and swollen, Jyotsna knew that must be the lingering effect of the drugs he had taken in the night. Jyotsna could read the language of lust in Ajay's eyes, the way he was looking at Elizabeth. She took the vegetables from Elizabeth and asked her to go home.

Ajay returned to his room disappointed, his face looking even more sinister than before. In the evening he was looking for Elizabeth, "to bring a glass of water to his room", but Jyotsna sent the water through Kamalesh. Ajay called Kajal to his room to teach her Maths, she refused to go. Ajay came out of his room and caught hold of Kajal, threatening her for insulting him with her refusal. She went crying to Jyotsna who pacified Ajay.

It was end of November, Daringibadi was turning colder. In the nights the animals were getting more active, howling all the time.

Ajay had been sleeping quite soundly for the last three nights, his after-dinner glass of milk being spiked with a couple of sleeping pills by Jyotsna. On the third night Jyotsna woke up. There was the sound of a pack of hyenas howling. She got curious; she had never seen a pack of hyenas. She opened the door in Ajay's room and went outside. The night was vibrant, with all kinds of sounds echoing from the nearby forest. All she could see was the trees swaying to a gentle wind. She tiptoed back to her room.

Around three in the morning she and Amaresh got up to the sound of a hyena howling close to the house. He wanted to go and check, she pulled him back,

"Must be Ajay trying to imitate the cry of a Hyena, go back to sleep chanting Namah Shivay, Namah Shivay."

✳ ✳ ✳

Three months have passed since that fateful night. Amaresh and his family have shifted to a rented house half a kilometre from their farm. They are still haunted by the heart-rending image of a young man of twenty two, shredded to pieces by a pack of hyenas. The kids are traumatised by the thought of how the hyenas had bitten off pieces of flesh from different parts of the body. Amaresh had a tough time explaining to Mantriji how Ajay had this habit of going into the open to smoke his charas despite being warned by him not to do so. Jyotsna tries her best to get over that unforgettable night - the darkness outside, the swaying trees, the sleeping Ajay and the half open door. She shudders at the thought of it and closes her eyes, chanting the Maha Mrutyunjay mantra!

GLOSSARY

Beti – Daughter

Charas – Cannabis

Daringibadi – A beautiful hill station in Odisha

Dupatta – The cloth used for covering the bosom of a girl

Maha Mrutyunjaya Mantra – The powerful mantra of Lord Shiva

Mantriji – Minister

Om Namah Shivaya – Chanting the mantra of Lord Shiva

Rajput – A person belonging to the warrior class

Theek hai – It's alright

13

OUR FRIEND GRUMBLENATH

On a fine, balmy evening I came across Radhanath while taking a stroll in the market. We had not met for quite a few months although we live in the same town. That's because we are separated by miles of broken down streets, crowded bazaars and tons of noise and pollution. He is in a way lucky, living in the outskirts "enjoying" less of the city life, whereas I get the full brunt of the chaos of urban life in the center of the city. Yet we move on, content with our daily dose of rice and fish curry.

Now, if I tell this to my friends from the college who are in my group of morning walkers, the first question they would ask is "Radhanath? Who Radhanath, which Radhanath?" In reply I would smile and say, "Radhanath! Don't you remember Grumblenath from our college days? The one who thought smiling was a cardinal sin and whose frown could tumble a crown?" Of course, Grumblenath they would remember and break into a huge riot of laughter.

Actually Radhanath is not a bad man as such, but he is different from others, very very different. If someone asks you or me, "Hello friend, how are you?" we would smile, nod and say, "I am fine, life moves on….How are you my friend? All well?" But Radhanath has a different approach to life, if you ask him how are things, his animal instincts would awaken and he would pounce on you like he was waiting for a chance like this, and you were the chosen pounce-victim of the day,

"So? Now only you remembered a poor friend like me? What were you doing all these days? Didn't you ever think of making a call to find out if this old man is still alive or not? You think you are the only one in this city who is busy? Others are just useless time-wasters? Why are you asking how I am doing? Do you really care, you big fish of the pond, do you care for the small fingerlings?"

This assault would obviously unnerve the startled friend. He would feel squeamish, and murmur,

"I was only asking about your wellbeing. Is everything ok with you?"

Radhanath would let out a torrent of grievances,

"What ok? How can I be ok? This wretched body is a storehouse of all ailments - high sugar, BP, cholesterol, heart issues, you name it, I have it. I wonder why God has given me so many problems in one single birth, couldn't He keep something for my next births also?............."

Grumblenath would go on and on. We often feel our friend makes a valiant effort to test our patience. Instead of reeling out the names of so many ailments, he could very well carry a xerox copy of the list in his pocket. Upon being asked, "how are you", he should hand over the list and leave, the proceedings of the tête-à-tête concluded in solemn silence.

In one such encounters I had ventured to ask him what kind of treatment he was undergoing and who was his doctor.

Grumblenath flared up, as if I had inadvertently sprinkled some red chili powder on his unsuspecting rump,

"Treatment? Hah, you are talking of treatment? Do you know what torture it is to subject oneself to treatment? And you are asking me which doctor? Is there one doctor you can go for your ailments? No Sir, times have changed. This is the age of super specialization. If you have problem in your foot one specialist will see your toe, another specialist will treat your little finger, a third one will look at your ankle. Each will charge you 500 rupees and prescribe at least a dozen tests to "rule out" all possible and impossible calamities like Meningitis, Hepatitis, Nephritis, Tuberculosis, Filariasis, and Thrombosis. Add Thyroid, Corona and Lipid profile to that, apart from tests for sugar, sodium, uric acid, potassium, magnesium, calcium. Fingers have to be x-rayed, ankle has to be subjected to MRI. It will be a neat package of ten thousand rupees for tests alone. So you go back to the doctor after a week with the test reports and return with a prescription for another five thousand rupees of medicine. You wish you had listened to your inner soul and applied some pain killer ointment on your foot after hot water fomentation. But the wife would not leave you alone, insisting on dragging you to the doctor and secretly enjoying your discomfiture. And these doctors? Let me tell you, they are a real pain in the @& $."

The three-lettered reference to a delicate part of human anatomy would make me smile, because Grumblenath has many pains in his @& $ ever since we knew him as a student. I would still try to reason with him,

"You are being unfair to doctors. They are a real dedicated lot. Call them any time during day or night, they will come if it is an emergency. They save thousands of lives through their treatment. And didn't you see how they and the wonderful nurses took care of millions of patients during Corona, putting their own lives in danger? In every profession there are a few rotten eggs. It's not fair to paint all of them as bad."

Grumblenath had started shaking his head. Obviously he had a different point of view,

"You know what happened three years back? I had a bit of chest pain and my wife Surabhi rushed me to the hospital. Before I knew anything the doctor had inserted three bamboos into my heart."

I was shocked, "Bamboos? What do you mean bamboos?"

Radhanath's face became distorted with anguish,

"Stents! That too imported ones, each costing one lakh fifteen thousand rupees. The total cost of operation came to five and half lakh rupees."

I was stunned, "Five and half lakh rupees? How did you manage to pay?"

Radhanath's anguished face had become red like an over-ripe tomato,

"Not me, I could not have paid out of the paltry pension of a retired professor. My son who works in TCS has included the parents in his insurance scheme. He extracted the amount from them with great difficulty. You should see how the insurance fellows are all sugar and honey when they canvass their policies, but they sound like hissing cobras if you claim any amount from them. You have to threaten them with consumer court, high court, Supreme Court before they cough up the money."

"But five and half lakh rupees is a lot of money!"

"Yes, since government hospitals are dens of infection you have no choice but to go to private, corporate hospitals. They are in the *business* of health care. If you as much as sneeze there, they will immediately catch you, admit you in the hospital, conduct a dozen tests and release you after prescribing simple Sinarest. But not before extracting a couple of lakhs from you. When I was getting the bamboo treatment from them I met a number of poor patients who had sold off their land in the village to arrange money for their treatment. If they get well they wouldn't know how to eke out a living, their land having been sold out. If they die, the relatives will have no money to take the body to the village and the hospital authorities will not release the body until the full cost of the treatment is paid. It is pathetic my friend, utterly pathetic. I don't know why the government can't open a good, modern hospital in every block headquarters and municipality to take care of our poor patients."

Having worked in government for more than thirty five years I have also often asked the question, but I am yet to find an answer to that.

The friends of Grumblenath know that he is a big critic of the government. Six months back I had met him in the market and asked him how was life; I hoped everything was going on well. He had growled,

"Well? How can it be well? We don't live in posh localities like you. If I had a house in Nayapalli, like you have, I wouldn't be suffering today. My scooter died three days back - a gory, untimely death. I have been going everywhere by walk. My poor chappals might also die soon."

I tried to cheer him up, "Don't talk of death so lightly. Didn't someone say, every death is a new beginning, when the night dies, morning is born, when darkness leaves light dawns. Count every new day as a blessing, then only life will be joyful. If your old chappals die new chappals will come to your life. Anyway, what happened to your scooter?"

"It died on the road on a rainy night, hitting a pothole. The ?&@??@ people call our city a smart city! A smart city - my @?&@@@&!"

I was taken aback, as if I had just been bitten by a playful monkey on my rump. I was in fact stunned by the severity of Radhanath's emotions. He had uttered two utterly unprintable words in quick succession and coming from his professorial mouth they sounded like two bomb explosions in a crowded market place. My eye brows shot up like the signals at a railway level crossing,

"How did your scooter hit a pothole? Was there no street light?"

Radhanath grimaced, like a drunk suddenly finding the shutters of the liquor shop pulled down,

"Street light? Are you serious or are you joking with this poor friend of yours? Don't you know, in this @&@?@& smart city the electricity board jokers switch off the power supply at the slightest hint of rains, or thunder?"

Recovering from the shock of a third expletive in less than three minutes coming like a loud shot from an well-oiled pistol, I realised Radhanath had inadvertently hit the nail on the electricity board's thick head. Having lived in different cities of the country for considerable lengths of time, I had never seen power connection being cut off at the hint of a rain or lightning. In fact, Mumbai, the excellent city, is never plunged into darkness even when the entire city is submerged in non-stop torrential rains. I have asked many friends why Bhubaneswar experiences this extraordinary phenomenon. But like many unresolved questions of life, this has remained an enigma.

Yet, I knew it was my duty to console Radhanath. After all, what were friends for if they couldn't put a little soothing balm on a painful monkey-bite? Moreover, Radhanath's eloquence in the matter of unprintable expletives had impressed me, almost to the point of a spiritual awakening. Such expletives were our daily fodder during the college days, but the way Radhanath uttered them with ease and élan, sort of shook me to my roots. I felt like complimenting him,

"Bah Radhanath, your command over the colourful language still remains fresh and young. Happy to note that. Don't worry, you will get back your scooter repaired, painted and shining like a recycled bride. At least you are lucky to own a scooter, look around you, there are so many who are walking or riding a bicycle. You................."

Grumblenath interrupted me, his irrepressible dark mood refused to see a streak of light,

"Lucky? What lucky? Look at those two guys walking on the pavement on the other side of the road, talking, nudging each other, sharing a bidi and rolling in laughter. And see the guy coming down the road on his bicycle, singing at the top of his voice. Ah, listen carefully, it is a romantic song for his sweetheart, who is probably waiting at the corner to hop on to his bicycle, and together they would ride on to everlasting happiness. They are the real lucky ones, always happy, laughing, singing their heart out. What do I have to feel happy?"

I smiled, "Don't be so modest, Radhanath. You have an apartment, a good wife, two devoted sons, a pension - you have worked diligently all these years, teaching young students, moulding their life. God has given you a happy, contented life - a reward for your good Karma."

Grumblenath exploded, as if a gas pipe in search of premature Nirvana, had managed to seduce a coy flame in a dark alley.

"Karma? What @&!&@ Karma? And what good deeds? You think all these have any meaning? In front of our apartment complex there is a palatial house. Massive building, big lawns, high compound walls, two big cars, one of them an SUV - we used to think some big industrialist lives there. One day we came to know that the person is a retired RTO. He goes abroad three four times a year, takes his wife on trips to Agra, Khajuraho, Kashmir and Bangalore. Look at us, we go to Puri, Konark, Chilika, stay at the cheapest hotels, eat junk and return home, drained of money and energy. My friend, there is no such thing as reward for good Karma. Otherwise how God would have been super kind to the RTO? His two sons are in US, floating in dollars. Look at my two sons - one is a poor lowly-paid engineer in TCS, the other is languishing as an agricultural officer in some remote corner of the state. And you say God is kind to good people. No, my friend, this is Kaliyug, sinners are winners, we are the losers."

I was not prepared to accept his argument that Radhanath's two sons were any less than his prosperous neighbour's sons. In fact we had seen them as growing boys and were impressed with their good manners. My wife Kalyani used to refer to them as two pieces of diamond. When Radhanath was posted as a lecturer at Dhenkanal we used to drop in at his place on the way back from Sambalpur where Kalyani's parents lived. His wife Surabhi was an excellent hostess, always welcoming us and feeding us the choicest dishes.

Once when we praised their two sons as pieces of diamond, Radhanath in his usual way grumbled, 'what diamonds - it is only through Surabhi's strenuous efforts that they came to our lives, otherwise who am I to claim any ownership over them?' Surabhi's face became red with deep embarrassment; she pinched him in his arm and managed to divert the topic. Kalyani and I had a roaring laughter on our drive back from Dhenkanal, speculating on the various kinds of strenuous efforts Surabhi would have taken for getting two precious pieces of diamond as their sons. We would stop, and in a few seconds Kalyani would start again, roaring with laughter till tears came out of her eyes.

✳✳✳

Three months after my unexpected evening meeting with Radhanath at the market, Kalyani cornered me one day after my return from morning walk. She looked concerned,

"Have you heard about the hospitalisation of Radhanath Babu?"

I was shocked, "Radhanath? Hospitalised? Why? What happened to him?"

"Your friend Dr. Hrudanand's wife called me a few minutes back. It seems Radhanath Babu was stabbed in the stomach three days back."

"O my God!" I exclaimed, "Three days back! That was Independence Day - who stabbed Radhanath on such a momentous day? Radhanath, of all the people, he is a nondescript poor chap, as harmless as a sozzled frog!"

"I have no idea, let's go and visit him. Poor Surabhi, she must be worried."

Radhanath turned his face away when I approached him in his cabin. His face had swollen like the backside of an abandoned Ambassador car, there were tubes going in and coming out of his body at all sorts of mentionable and unmentionable places. Kalyani, who has a delicate heart, could not stand the sight of the heavily bandaged Radhanath sprawled helplessly on the hospital bed. She went out with Surabhi. My heart swelled with pity, looking at my suffering friend. In a trembling voice I asked him how he was feeling. I was surprised at his reaction. His voice was weak, but the words were strong,

"So? You could find time finally, after three days? I almost died, and you did not think of visiting me even once all these days? You think only big shots like you deserve to live and poor professors should kick the bucket and leave the world…….."

I cut him short, "Listen, we will go into that later, first tell me how you are feeling and how did you land up in this ghastly place?"

"I am feeling weak, drained out, but I think I will survive."

"Of course you will survive. But tell me what happened?"

Radhanath was surprised at my ignorance. He got back some of his spirit,

"Didn't you read it in the newspapers? It was all over the town. For a couple of days I became famous. TV cameras, reporters, journalists, the whole zing bang crowd. I almost thought someone will make a movie on me and offer me the lead role."

I couldn't suppress a smile. Radhanath would be a box office hit as a hero if he would be allowed to use the kind of free speech he used the other day! I shook my head,

"No, we are getting our house painted, no time to read the newspapers. I even don't know where they disappear in the morning. Our TV is also tucked away somewhere wrapped in clean bed sheets. You have to tell me what happened to you"

Radhanath made a strenuous effort to sit up. He beckoned me to give him some water. I did.

"On the morning of 15th August, the Independence Day, I left for my daily four-kilometres walk. You of course know our smart city actually belongs to street dogs and humans are unwanted intruders in their howling lives. In fact it's a city for the dogs, by the dogs, of the dogs, a sort of dogocractic paradise for the four legged beasts. So one cannot walk on the pavements for fear of treading on the overflowing dog poop, and we are forced to walk on the streets, always on the watch for overspeeding bikes and evil looking, demonic dogs. I was walking and talking on the mobile phone glued to my ear. Suddenly two @&?!&@ bastards came from behind on a motorbike, one of them snatched my phone and they tried to speed away. But just a couple of meters away there was a ditch and their bike skidded on that. I pounced on the @&??!@ boy sitting on the pillion, he had fallen down, the other &?!@!& boy of doubtful parentage was struggling to straighten the bike. He managed to rev up its engine and moved a little forward. Do you see that nice-looking stick lying on the table there?"

I turned my head and saw the object of Grumblenath's admiration. It was indeed a cutie, lying there smug and full of self-pride like someone who had just cleared UPSC's Civil Services Exam and waiting for parents of nubile brides queuing up before him for sumptuous matri-money for their daughters. My heart had perked up considerably, noticing how Radhanath's spirit had not diminished even a wee bit and he was spewing colourful expletives like a wily magician throwing knives into the air. Radhanath smiled, although on his heavily camouflaged face tied with bandage, the smile looked like a grimace,

"With that blessed stick, which I always carry during my walk, to ward off enthusiastic dogs taking an unnatural fancy to my hindquarters, I gave the boy some of the best and juiciest beating you can imagine. He was begging for mercy, having thrown away the mobile phone to the roadside. But I was seized with a maniacal anger. I kept beating him as if that would bring me a ticket to fly to the moon. And I kept shouting at the two @&?!@ bastards, "You bloody scoundrels, you &??@!?? and &?@?!??&@, what do you think of us? Your helpless preys? On Independence Day we innocent citizens don't have the freedom to walk peacefully on the street and you @&??&@ have the freedom to steal, loot, rape and murder? Is this why the country got independence, to let you loose among innocent people like hungry wolves on a pack of deers? I will kill this @&?@&? today, let me first smash his bones to pieces......" The boy on the ground started crying, the one on the motorbike kept shouting, "Uncle, uncle, let him go, don't ask for trouble, you will regret it." I kept beating the boy, who was now rolling on the ground in pain. Suddenly the boy on the bike got down, took out a knife and stabbed me two times on the stomach. Blood oozed out like a soda fountain. I grabbed my stomach and fell on the road. The two boys sped away. Some of the onlookers who had watched the tamasha without raising their finger, rushed to me. Someone called the police and the ambulance. I had lost a lot of blood, the cut was deep. I had lost consciousness. The doctors must have done a good job, the young and cute nurses are all kind and sweet to me, why should they not be? I must be looking innocent and harmless like their grandfathers."

Radhanath smiled again, remembering the young and cute nurses. I joined him in his smilothon,

"So you don't have grudges against the doctors anymore? After all they saved your life!"

Radhanath looked at me with a sort of piercing gaze,

"Doctors? Blast the doctors! Who cares for them? Look at where the country is heading. Even on a sacred day like Independence Day, there is no law and order in the state capital, no fear for police. Goons are out to rob the innocent citizens in open daylight. My friend, our country has gone to dogs. Lawlessness, indiscipline, corruption, dishonesty - all these have pushed the country to a sorrowful abyss. There is need for a fresh revolution to rescue the country. You know when I regained my consciousness and was told that I had lost more than ten ounces of blood, what I said to myself?"

I shook my head, there was no way I could have known what Radhanath told himself.

The words that followed from our perennial iconoclast Grumblenath left me stunned,

"You know, somehow I thought the country is in need of a new revolution and to free it from the bondage of lawlessness and corruption, ten ounces of blood are nothing, I am prepared to lay down my life for the cause."

GLOSSARY

Chappal – A commonly used footwear

Kaliyug – According to Hindu mythology there are four celestial eras – Kaliyug is the current one

– 14 –

THE STREAM OF UNCONSCIOUSNESS

The room had become stiflingly hot. The sky outside was overcast and humidity had reached its peak. Sadanand desperately wanted a glass of soft drink with lot of ice. The small hotel at Jaipur, the capital city of Rajasthan, had gone to sleep, it was close to eleven in the night. Water in the jug in the hotel room had become warm. He just couldn't resist the temptation to go out for a soft drink. And he knew rain was imminent. Coming from the desert district of Barhmer, where it rains probably half a dozen times in the year, the desire to get drenched was compulsive. He went out.

The watchman was dozing at the main door. Sadanand asked him if there was a shop nearby selling coca cola. The watchman yawned and tried to smile, a difficult task, considering that more than half his face was covered with a huge moustache, looking like the wings of a gargantuan butterfly.

"Sahab, it is close to eleven, all the shops near this place will be closed. If you are really desperate for coca cola, you have to walk about one and half kilometres. There is an all-night bazar where some shops sell coca cola and all kinds of drinks."

"But, what kind of bazar is that, open throughout the night? Don't those people sleep in the night?"

The watchman laughed,

"O, no, no, they work in the night and sleep during the day."

Sadanand was shocked,

"Who are these shop keepers? What do they sell?"

"Arey Sahab, you are too innocent. People from Barhmer are like that. I am from Jaisalmer. I was also like you when I came here. Now I know who sells what in different bazaars of Jaipur. Now you go and buy your coca cola and come back here. Don't enter that bazar. That is not for decent people like you."

"Ok, can you give some direction?"

"Yes, that is easy. Once you go out of the compound here, take a right turn, go straight for half a kilometre till you reach a petrol bunk. You will see a fork in the road there, take the left one and keep going. After a kilometre you will see the lights of the shop. They keep the area well decorated to attract the customers. But remember," the watchman shook his fingers, "no going inside the bazar. Just buy the coca cola and come back."

Sadanand nodded and started walking. The air was getting cooler. Ah, rains are so beautiful! At Barhmer where he worked as a lecturer in the local college, rains were rare and when they came it never poured. He wished he would succeed in the interview for the post of Lecturer at Jaipur University and come to live here with his wife Sucheta, son Dushyant and daughter Dikshita! He remembered how the six months old Dikshita had grabbed his fingers with her tiny hand, as if pleading with him not to leave her and go away for three days.

Lights were on in some of the houses. People were watching TV. He missed Sucheta, who must be still glued to the TV playing some stupid serial or the other. She was fiercely addicted to serials. And every night he pleaded with her to come to bed early,

"How can you let yourself be fooled by the never-ending episodes, the hero dying and getting resurrected, the heroine becoming a ghost in the night and a seductress during the day, the dance, songs going on for years without the actors and actresses dying of fatigue!"

She would get vocal,

"Why are you after my serials? Are you a 'serial killer'? Go and sleep, if you want something from me, then wait. Haven't you heard the saying, the fruit of patience is sweet?"

"Ok, I will wait here for the sweet fruit of patience. You watch TV, I will watch you watching TV."

After five minutes she would shout at him in mock anger,

"Don't keep looking at me like a hungry wolf! I am getting distracted, not able to concentrate on my serial!"

Sadanand would go to the bed room and keep tossing and turning on the bed waiting for her. He loved Sucheta. She was an excellent wife; she took good care of his parents who often came from the village to stay with their only child. In fact Sadanand and Sucheta were planning to have them permanently at Jaipur in case he got the job at the university. He wished he would succeed in the interview that was to take place two days later.

The shops were visible now, all lighted and decorated. Sadanand reached the place and was surprised to see so much activity, although it was past eleven. There were about a dozen shops with exotic names, "Raat Ki Raani", "Dil Baahaar", "Jannat Ki Husn" "Manoranjan" and absurd names like "Nani Yaad Aa Jayegi", to "Ek Baar To Chakhle". He crossed the road to the other side and a few shops away he found a big crowd. The name of the shop was "Dil Khush Lassi- Binnoo Pehelwan Ki World Famous Dukan".

Sadanand went there and asked if he could get a glass of coca cola with lots of ice. Binnoo Pehelwan laughed and was joined by a couple of other customers,

"Are you from outside of Jaipur?"

"Yes, I am from Barhmer, but what has it got to do with coca cola?"

"That's why you are asking for coca cola in Binnoo Pehelwan' Dukan, it's like asking for a kilo of Bhindi in a mutton shop"

He broke into a big laugh and as if on cue, few others also laughed loudly,

"Arey Sahab, forget coca cola, taste a glass of special lassi from here, you will never forget it in your life. And if you find better lassi than mine anywhere in Rajasthan, come back here, I will give you a full refund of the thirty rupees I am going to charge you. Arey Chhotu, make a glass of special lassi for Sahab."

Sadanand smiled and sat on a bench waiting for his glass of lassi. A couple of people sitting there moved and made space for him. One of them smiled and asked,

"Are you an afsar?"

"No I am a.........", Sadanand was about to say Lecturer, but realised the word would be unknown to these people, so he simply said, "a master"

Binnoo Pehelwan offered a tall glass of lassi and said,

"Masterji, here is your lassi, enjoy. I am sure you will go back and tell everyone in Barhmer about it."

Sadanand took a sip, it was delicious; he had never tasted anything like that in his life,

"Pehelwanji, this is extraordinary, how do you make such fantastic lassi?"

Binnoo Pehelwan laughed,

"It's a trade secret; you will remember the taste till you reach Barhmer"

Everyone had a good laugh.

Sadanand finished the lassi, paid for it and left. Through a road on the side of the shop customers were entering the bazar, with a spring in their steps, cheap perfume wafting through the air like the tune of a haunting song. He avoided the side road and crossed to the other side. The air was much cooler, Sadanand felt light in the head. He tried to locate the road which had brought him to that point, but there were many roads and he forgot which one he had taken. He walked a bit and got confused. Somehow it made him laugh. Such a simple task, and he was unable to do it! He laughed loudly and kept laughing. Suddenly he shouted "Tchah! What a ..." he groped for the right word, shame? Joke? Then he remembered he often called his Dushyant the son of a gun, Bandhook Ka

Bacha! So his face lighted up, he repeated "Tchah! What a Bandhook!" He liked that a lot, in fact he liked it more than anything he had said in life! So he stood there, laughed again and said "Tchah! What a Bandhook!" He liked his voice saying that and repeated "Tchah! What a Bandhook!" After he had laughed and said it six times, he suddenly became conscious, what is this, why was he doing it, past twelve o clock on an August night in Jaipur, he, a loving husband to a beautiful wife, a responsible father to two adorable kids, a respectable Guruji to his students?

He decided to move on, he thought he found the road he had taken and started walking on it. His mind was still grappling with the mystery of why he stood on the road and shouted like a crazy man. He wanted to upbraid himself for that, so he hit his forehead with the palm and said, "Tchah, what a Bandhook!"

He bit his tongue in embarrassment realising that he repeated exactly what had embarrassed him earlier, so he smiled and walked on. The smile came back to him again and again like mild streaks of lightning but he didn't stop.

A hundred meters on he entered a lane which was lighted like it was day time, bright street lights were on, people were sitting outside on their string beds and chatting, some were smoking from their hookahs. Suddenly a small girl came running from the side and collided with his leg. Sadanand stood there mortified, afraid the girl would start crying and her parents would scold him, but the girl started giggling. She took his hand and dragged him to under a tree where her parents were sitting. There was a baby in a stroller, the girl said,

"Uncle, uncle, look at my brother Golu, isn't he the most handsome kid on earth?"

Sadanand looked at the boy, he must be around seven or eight months of age, he was laughing and throwing his legs in the air. He was indeed quite cute, Sadanand remembered his daughter, how she had grabbed his finger tightly when he was taking leave from her. His heart brimmed with unbridled love for Golu, the boy in the stroller. He asked the parents if he could hold the baby as he reminded him of his six months old daughter back home at Barhmer. They smiled and said of course! Sadanand took the boy in his arms, he had never felt so much love in his life, it was as if the baby became a part of his heart, his soul and his existence, as if it was a baby God he was holding in his arms. He pressed him to his chest and started kissing him on the cheeks, the forehead and the hair. The baby started squirming, smothered by so much love. The parents started wondering what had possessed the unknown man, why he was overflowing with love for the child. Sadanand had no idea about their discomfort; he kept on kissing the baby boy and pressing him to his chest. The mother nodded at her husband to rescue the baby, he came and quietly took the baby from the clutches of Sadanand and put him back in the stroller.

"Where are you going Bhai Sahab, so late in the night?"

Sadanand looked at him, trying to remember the name of the hotel. He finally remembered it,

"Raj Tarangini Guest House, that's where I am staying."

"Do you know the way to that place?"

Sadanand laughed, a little too loudly, startling the small girl,

"Yes, of course"

And he muttered to himself "Tchah, what a Bandhook!" and started walking. The girl called after him, "Uncle, Please come tomorrow again, to see my Golu."

Sadanand waved at her.

A couple of hundred meters from there he saw an open space where a few boys were playing football. They were around eight-nine years old, some of them were bare bodied, some had coloured banyans on. He looked at them and thought of Dushyant who had already started playing with a football at the age of six. In a couple of years Dushyant would also play football with his friends. Sadanand wanted to play with the kids. But he knew he had to pretend to be Dushyant to be accepted by them. He went near them,

"Hi kids, will you allow me to play with you?"

"But uncle you are so big, if you kick one of us, we will fly in the air!"

"No no, I am not big, I am only six years old, call me Dushyant, don't call me uncle".

"Ok uncle, you can play with us, but be careful, don't kick any of us."

"No, no, not uncle, only Dushyant, call me Dushyant!"

The kids found it fun to shout at 'Dushyant', 'Hey Dushyant, pass the ball, Dushyant, kick the ball to the goal, Dushyant, here, to the right………"

Sadanand was having a ball, the best time of his life. He wanted to show to the kids how Ronaldinho dribbled, how Messi headed the ball, how Ronaldo shot his free kicks…… soon the boys stood and clapped when Sadanand ran with the ball from one end to the other and scored goal after goal.........He became a hero to the kids and it appeared to him that the flats all around the open space were stands in a huge stadium and thousands of spectators were shouting, cheering him and clapping at the goals he scored. The adulation was heady, the lightness in his head felt even lighter. He stopped after a few minutes, shook hands with each of the boys like an international player taking leave from his team mates. He waved at the spectators in the stadium and left the field in a blaze of glory. He hadn't felt so happy over a football game for so many years. From somewhere he heard the song O Basanti Pawan Pagal playing, he looked around to see from which house it was coming. To his utter surprise he found the song playing in his heart, as if from a transistor. He laughed to himself and said loudly, "Tchah, what a Bandhook!" and walked on.

Down the road he came across a park to his right. It was well-manicured, beautiful trees swayed in the cool breeze under subdued lights. He entered inside and was pleasantly surprised to see many young couples sitting on the benches under the trees and chatting, holding hands, looking into each other's eyes. At a dark corner he saw a young boy and girl who looked like school kids, in an intimate embrace, kissing each other. The front buttons of the girl's dress were open and she had closed her eyes. Sadanand felt so angry, so frightfully angry! What kind of kids are these! Taking such liberties in a park! He shouted at them,

"Hey, do your parents know you are doing these dirty things here?"

The young pair got up, shocked, the girl arranged her dress and stood there, her head bent. Sadanand went to a tree, broke a branch and came menacingly at them. They started running, Sadanand's anger was like a fire from a furnace, soon it had spread to other corners of the park, there was pandemonium all around. Young men and women, boys and girls started running away from the park, Sadanand chased each of them giving a blow or two to a few with the improvised lathi. Soon the park was empty, but Sadanand's anger had not abated. He kept cursing the "characterless youth" under his breath as he walked away from the park.

It was well beyond midnight then, approaching one o clock. He suddenly saw a few people sitting in a row on the roads. They were obviously quite poor, begging for money. He went to an old couple and asked them what they were doing so late in the night,

"It's not late night, Babu; it's early morning. There is a Hanuman temple in the adjoining lane, by four the devotees start coming. They give good alms Babu, but the regular beggars don't allow us near the temple. We are not beggars. There are about a dozen of us here, all abandoned by the children. They don't take care of us anymore. Our son lives in Delhi and daughter is in our village but they have told us to fend for ourselves. What can I do Babu at this age, I am eighty four, my old lady is seventy six. Who will give us work? So we live here under the sky, waiting for some alms from the devotees. Look at these people sleeping, they are all destitutes. There is no one to take care of them. Give us something babu, it will buy us a meal in the morning. We haven't eaten anything for more than twelve hours."

Sadanand's anger had subsided, the tale of woe of these destitutes melted his heart. Some others had woken up from their light sleep and were looking expectantly at him.

He took out all the money he had in his pocket and counted it - eighty seven rupees. He gave it to them and asked them to share it among themselves. They blessed him. His eyes filled with tears, when he started walking away from them. Somehow he imagined that one day he and Sucheta would be old and may be destitutes like this, abandoned by their children who would be in far off places. Sucheta and he would be sitting near some temple and begging for their next meal. Uncontrolled waves of agony racked his body and he started sobbing.

The path he walked on was meandering into some sort of a deserted area, dark and grim. By the time the sobbing subsided he was suddenly aware of some light flickering behind him. He looked back and was astounded to see a procession of some people walking with torches of flame in their hand. It was a silent procession and as it drew near he saw a dead body being carried on the shoulders of six men. A few others were accompanying them, all with a torch of flame in their hands, walking silently. In no time they overtook him. He was shocked, why was a funeral procession marching past midnight? Whose body was that? Why was there no chanting of Ram Naam Satya Hai? Why was the procession so silent? He moved a bit faster and tapped on the shoulder of the hind most man carrying the body, to ask him whose body was that. When the man turned, Sadanand froze in fear, a cold terror gripping his heart. It was the watchman with the big moustache from the Raj Tarangini Guest House, who shook his fingers, forbidding him to ask any questions, the way he had forbidden him to go into the lighted bazar a few hours back. When the man next to the watchman looked at Sadanand, his heart sank. What was Binnoo Pehelwan doing here, why was he not at his shop selling his world famous lassi? One by one the other four also looked back. They all looked familiar, friends and colleagues from his college in Barhmer!

Sadanand froze in terror, his legs refused to move, he let the procession go ahead. He wanted to go back on the way he had come. When he turned, he got another big shock. All the street lights had gone off, it was dark, densely dark as if he was staring at a closed tunnel. He was scared to go back. He resumed his walk and after fifty meters or so the road ended in a big ground, sort of an old park. He entered it and looked around. His mind had stopped registering much. In the faint light of the moon peeping shyly from behind the clouds he could see the outline of some fences encircling the ground, he thought it could be a park, a playground, patch of a desert, or even a fragment of the sky. He didn't care anymore. He just wanted to lie down where he stood. He looked up at the sky, dark, ominous clouds gradually overtook it like a black canopy, hiding the moon. The first drops of a slight drizzle started falling. As he sat down on the grass and tumbled over to curl into a sleep, he wondered if he would ever get up again, he felt his cute daughter's tiny hand gripping his fingers and trying to pull him back from some unknown precipice.

The drizzle came, but by a miracle a wind swept away the clouds and the rain stopped. The moon reappeared and shone upon the lone figure of a dazed Sadanand deep asleep in the open ground. With the sun shining bright and hot in the morning Sadanand woke up. He didn't know where he was and wondered why he was out in the open in a park, with cows and goats for company. He dimly saw a group approaching him. A man was walking with a stroller, a small girl running by his side. The man saw him and stopped, surprise clouding his face,

"Bhai Saab, is it you? What are you doing here? Didn't you reach your hotel last night?"

The girl tried to pull him up,

"Uncle, uncle, come and see my Golu, isn't he the cutest baby on earth?"

Sadanand looked at the man, embarrassed. He himself wondered how he ended up in this open field last night. The last thing he remembered was a funeral procession and darkness all around him.

He shook his head in reply,

"Sorry Bhai Saab, I don't know how I came here, I clearly remember I was going back to my hotel!"

The man looked at him closely,

"Where were you before you met us near our home? What were you doing so late in the evening outside your hotel?"

"I had come to have some cocacola with lots of ice, it was so stiflingly hot in the hotel room, but someone persuaded me to have some lassi instead!"

"O my God, did you have the special lassi in the famous shop of Binnoo Pehelwan?"

Sadanand nodded, remembering the wonderful taste of the lassi last night.

The man patted his head with his hand,

"O my God, O my God, was it the first time you ever had a special lassi? Didn't you know special lassi comes laced with a liberal dose of Bhang? Why did you do that in an unknown place in a deserted town?"

Sadanand smiled, he was no doubt happy to be alive after a heart-wrenching ordeal,

"What do I know? I had come out of the hotel looking for a glass of cold coca cola. Did I know, in one single, unforgettable night I would see a procession of life before my eyes? A life complete with the joys of infancy, childhood, adolescence, youth and then soaked with the sorrow of destitution and death?"

***

Author's Note:

In November 1989, I drank a glass of lassi with Bhang, for the first time in my life, on a Diwali evening at a party in Chennai. I was curious to know how it felt. The friends egged me on and I took a liberal quantity of lassi with bhang. In no time I was laughing like a demon possessed and was eventually packed off home in the company of my family. In a span of the next one and half hours I experienced a kaleidoscope of emotions in a frighteningly severe intensity - joy, affection, anger, sorrow and fear, all of which I have tried to describe in the above story. Even today I clearly remember the song "O Basanti Pawan Pagal' playing inside my heart, yes, believe it or not, it was as if a record player was on somewhere inside my heart playing that song. When I came out to lock the front gate of our house, I was certain that someone was hiding there with a knife to attack me. My wife somehow made me go to sleep. I woke up the next evening after fourteen hours, relatively sober and free from the effect of bhang. I have never touched the weird stuff again.

GLOSSARY

Afsar – Officer

Bandhuk – Gun

Barhmer – A desert district of Rajasthan

Bhang – A paste of highly intoxicating Cannabis leaves

Dil Bahaar – Scented air warming up the heart

Dil Khush – Filling the heart with joy

Dukan – Shop

Ek Baar To Chakhle – Taste it at least once

Jannat Ki Husn – Heavenly Beauty

Lassi – Sweetened buttermilk

Lathi – A thick stick used for beating

Manoranjan – Entertainment

Naani Yaad Aa Jayegi – One will remember his Grandma

Pehelwan – Wrestler

Raat Ki Raani – Queen of the night

– 15 –

THE BROKEN PUMPSET

In the evening of life, as one sits down to ruminate over the many experiences of life, the thing that stands out as a sore thumb is the lost opportunity of our great country to live up to its potential. Otherwise how does one explain our media's obsession with Rhea Chakravorty's alleged drug procurement for her live-in partner or the timing of Baby Taimur Khan's princely burp, when China is building up its armaments pile, snooping on India's who's who or strengthening its communication network in Ladakh preparing for a royal backstabbing while pretending to go through the motion of peace talks? And to make matters worse, the spectre of unemployment, lack of income, hunger and poverty is likely to ravage the country for decades to come! We talk of minimum governance and ease of doing business, yet ask anyone, who has to visit a government office and he would tell you nothing has changed.

Every time I think in these lines I remember an anecdote narrated to me by a senior colleague from one of the big states of Northern India.

It was sometime in the year 2010. I was working as Additional Secretary in Cabinet Secretariat. This senior colleague was a Secretary to Government of India and used to drop in for a chat once in a while. We used to discuss issues of governance and he narrated to me an interesting experience of his. He told me, his family owned some sizeable agricultural land in his ancestral village in the state where he had served as a senior IAS officer before coming to the Government of India on deputation. He used to visit his village once in three months to check on the land. During one such visit, the villagers complained that they were not getting water for the past two months from the overhead tank since the motor in the pump set had burnt out. They had approached the local authorities, but had got no relief.

The Officer took out his mobile phone promptly and called the DM of the district in the presence of the villagers.

"DM Saab, I am xxxx, visiting my village xxxx in xxxx Tehsil. People here are complaining that the pump set for the overhead tank is not working for the past three months. Can you please get it fixed?"

"Yes Sir, such a small matter, and you had to take the trouble of calling! Consider it done sir. I will give instructions today itself!"

The villagers were thrilled. However nothing happened, the pump set remained in a daze without a motor to bring it to life. One of the villagers called the Officer in Delhi. He contacted the DM again, was again assured that the work would be done. Still nothing happened. The Officer then called the Divisional Commissioner who was respectful, but the respect did not translate into action. Finally, the Chief Secretary, the Officer's batchmate in IAS and a close friend, assured him action after giving a mouthful for being disturbed on such a trivial issue. But the pump set still remained in hibernation, soaked in the memory of its past glory. No one from the village called again, so the Officer assumed that the pump set had returned to life and was doing what it was meant to do, namely, pumping water to the overhead tank.

When the Officer visited the village after a few months he was shocked to learn that nothing had happened, no one from the Sarkar Bahadur had visited the village to take a look at the forlorn pump set, lying abandoned in a corner like a terminally ill patient. The Officer was at his wits' end, wondering what to do next, when in the market of the nearby town he came across the Mukhiya of another big village. This humble servant of the people was actually a Don and quite high in the hierarchy of Dons because of the twenty odd murder cases pending against him. He greeted our Officer and asked about his haalchaal (goings on). The Officer, by a sudden inspiration, narrated the ordeals of the villagers. The Mukhiya raised his surprised eyebrows and mocked at the Officer's naïveté in assuming that in his exalted state works got done by approaching DMs. and Chief Secretaries.

The Don went on to demonstrate the true modus operandi of governance. He got down from his jeep and sent his two gunmen "to go and lift the JE (Junior Engineer) from wherever he is and bring him to Saab's village". He got into the Officer's car and they went to the overhead tank where the pump set was languishing. He asked some of the villagers to bring a charpai (a string cot), clean bed sheet and a pillow. In about an hour the gunmen produced the JE of the Block office. The Don greeted him and gave the necessary instructions to the trembling official with the following words,

"JE Saab, welcome to this humble village. You are going to be the guest of the village for some time. I have made arrangements for you to stay in this pump house till the pump set is repaired. Look at the bed, this is where you will sit and work, don't even think of escaping. I am leaving my two gunmen here, they will shoot you if you try that. I will personally ensure that your dead body will be buried at a place where no one will find it. Now get busy, call whoever you want to and get the necessary stuff to repair the pump set. But remember you are not leaving this room till the villagers get water from the overhead tank."

The Officer cut the story short and with a big smirk told me that by evening the pump set was replaced with a new one and the JE went home. Over our humble cup of tea we had learnt a good lesson in governance.

Although difficult to believe, I have reproduced the story exactly as told to me by my senior colleague. If true, there are many takeaways from it, the most important being the indifference in the response system of officials at the helm of affairs. And as the officer told me, imagine, if this could happen to him what would be the plight of a common man seeking some relief from the mighty government?

I still wonder if we have found the answer to this simple question.

GLOSSARY

Sarkar Bahadur – The big government

Mukhiya – Headman of a village

OTHER BOOKS BY MRUTYUNJAY SARANGI

1. JASMINE GIRL AT HAJI ALI AND OTHER STORIES

(February 2022)

Published by Mrutyunjay Sarangi

Price Rs. 225 (Including postage)

Contact: +919930739537 or mrutyunjays@gmail.com

2. A TRAIN TO KOLKATA AND OTHER STORIES

(February 2022)

Published by Mrutyunjay Sarangi

Price Rs. 225 (Including postage)

Contact: +919930739537 or mrutyunjays@gmail.com

3. THE FOURTH MONKEY: A COLLECTION OF SHORT STORIES

(May 2023)

Published by Notion Press, Chennai.

Price Rs. 249

Available on Notionpress.com/store,

Amazon.in and Flipkart.in

Also available internationally on Amazon.com and in Ebook versions

Contact: +919930739537 or mrutyunjays@gmail.com